Micha[illegible]

Joy in [illegible]

for not [illegible]

being. Blessings on your journey

ever deepening. Love, Carole Ann

mother

STORIES

Through our Mothers' Death and Dying

Shirley —

What a delight to know

you - my heart is always open

to new friends much love,

CAROLE ANN DRICK Carole Ann

7-22-13

ISBN: 1-4196-8981-9
ISBN-13: 9781419689819

Visit www.booksurge.com to order additional copies.

T0 MY FAMILY

Kimberly L. Kimbrough
Janet Marie Thomae-Shaulis
Shawn Shaulis
Mason Shaulis
Philip Cotter
Miranda Toups
Elizabeth Bachofer
Vessel
Sheila Cagle
Patt Thomas
Lynn Keegan
Virgil

For your unconditional love & support my deepest gratitude.

TO EVERYONE WHO READS THIS BOOK

My gratitude for exploring our prospering world beyond time and space.

CONTENTS

ACKNOWLEDGEMENTS

To all the daughters who have mothers, which I have reason to believe we all have – for their pondering of life and death and touching this inner world silently feeling there was something more and usually feeling that they were alone. Now is the time and here is the place, we take their innermost thoughts and begin to put them into a form that can be shared with others to discover that there really is more, much more beyond the physical loss of form.

To these women who have bravely stepped out to share their personal stories, their tears, their insights, their speaking from their heart has given to so many women a glimpse of the eternal.

To all those who come to me for personal facilitation through transition and death, whatever form it may take – thank you so much for leading the way by your example.

From love's deep connection,
thank you one and all.

PREFACE

On an early spring morning two years after my mother's physical death, I was sitting with Miranda Toups enjoying a cup of tea. Our gentle meanderings soon turned to our mothers' dying. Miranda's mother had died 3 years prior to mine and she was there to love and support her mother during the process. Our heart-felt sharing soon led to the power, insight and wisdom that our mothers' had given us not just throughout our lives, but in these final days of their lives and in their deaths. These were actually powerful gifts and realizations that we had with the final one being their deaths.

We sat in stillness as the realization began to sink in. Simultaneously we looked at each other exclaiming, "This is powerful.... Those are the final gifts.... Our inheritance." The small lingering strings of loss of the physical presence gave way to a yet deeper realization of the truth of the experience.

Miranda emphatically laughed her loud native Texas woman's laugh – long and deep. "Yes, and you need to write a book about it – and I have just the title, "Mother Stories." She paused, leaned forward and said, "And, have I got the story for you!"

Looking at her and feeling the rising awareness of the truth just spoken, I nodded, quietly answering, "Yes."

Mother Stories was born.

But how do we encourage women to look deeper and discover the cup is really half full? I started talking to family and friends. The idea was relished but no one felt they were a writer. Story telling became the key phrase to describe the writing process… women simply writing as if they were sitting across the table from me having a cup of tea and sharing their insights. Women writing from their hearts and discovering through the pain and sadness that there are incredible gifts and insights their mother has given them no matter the circumstances. These gifts are precious whether large or small – not only to them but also to other women. To assist yourself and others to see these gifts, accept the gifts, live the gifts, is to pass on a legacy of insight, feeling and awareness that empowers all women, all daughters, all mothers, all generations.

Although many opened their hearts to write, less than half submitted their story. The phone calls and emails usually started with some form of, "I really love this idea and really want to do this, but I can't get started" or "I'm not ready"… "This brings up so many things I didn't realize were there"… "It's too hard"…. "I don't want to go there again"… "I'm finished with that part of my life." Any yet, the brave women who did complete their story said they were "stronger… felt great peace, were walking in greater wisdom, moving with a power and Presence they had not known before."

Their insights, their energy of creation and sharing flows through me as I write these words. These powerful women from diverse ways of life have come together to offer you a glimpse of the movement from the world of form into the world of the formless, the world of God.

Regretfully, Miranda unexpectedly died before she could share her story.

Richard Back in *Illusions* so simply stated, "There is no problem without a gift in its hands. You have the problem because you need the gift."

So here we are sharing, sharing our stories - simple, direct, heart felt. There is no analysis, no interpretation. Each story stands by itself – written from the heart. And just maybe, there is a story or two that touches your deeper truth, that encourages you to go deeper and touch the hurt and moving beyond it discover your power, your wisdom, your mother's final gifts.

INTRODUCTION

The hole in life that occurs with physical death is like no other – permanent, irrevocable. In retrospect it seems like a great mystery, one minute the person is alive, talking and the next minute the physical body is lifeless. There is no more talking, sharing, arguing or laughing. The life force is gone. How can that be? Death can be very strange.

It could be said that the death of a woman's mother is quite possibly the deepest hole, leaving a strange sense of elder wisdom loss, a loss of the feminine wisdom, creativity and understanding. Knowing these attributes are in everyone, they are most readily personified in women.

When you finally go into the hurt, the pain of loss, and really go deep into the feeling, it feels like it might consume you. But no, when you actually go so deep that you touch the ache, you touch the pain, you can let go of all the resistance to what is. And then, there is an opening – a space. The peace, the grace comes rushing in flooding your entire being. Yes, the hurt is still there, but this space of physical emptiness becomes transmuted. It is like alchemy of transforming base metal into gold. The hole becomes the spiritual space that surrounds and enfolds us in

Presence. This grace, this sense of peace is a growing awareness of a steady ever flowing stream of life, a stream of great inner strength. And from this life stream the gifts of authentic wisdom and awareness begin to emerge.

In this sacred process called death the physical form both inside and outside is removed. In some ways it can be liberating to see the end of form; to realize after the form is gone the spirit, the vibration, continues. In time all physical things dissolve. With each death we are reminded that nothing last, nothing is permanent. We discover that something even as simple as our breath comes from the formless. It manifests for a brief period and then returns to the formless. This is a simple death but one that is repeated countless times over a lifetime. It is a continual gentle reminder that nothing lasts in physical form forever.

Death opens a small space beyond form in the fabric of existence. Every death is sacred and can be an incredible experience both for the one dying and for those remaining. Certainly one is in the presence of a great mystery. As you move beyond these stories you can feel and know for yourself the underlying Truth of who you really are. In a way we are all dying each day to the false physical self and that in itself is quite a beautiful thing.

Mother Stories are like gifts unbidden… full of surprise and delight while touching the heart. There are two words, Chi and Ohm, which speak of the vital Life Force that flows through each living thing. This vital Life Force is the universal connection that we all share... a river of life flowing through our bodies. Our delight is in sharing these stories to help bring alive the essence of these words in your being. This essence is pleading with us to slow down, to go within, to be still, to awaken once again to the great mystery of life that surrounds, enfolds, and is who we are.

Mother Stories are actually two gifts in one. The authors have received a tremendous gift in moving past the pain of physical loss into a place of peace and joy only to discover the incredible gifts that their mother's dying and death has given them. Gifts are only precious and increase in value when they are shared. In return these women have passed these insights as gifts onto you, the reader.

The hard part is attempting to move beyond the physical pain of loss and grief. Your heart feels this with each story. The best part is realizing the gifts, feeling the gifts of spirit that are coming through. You feel this as your heart opens even wider into and becomes the heart of God.

Warm regards,

Carole Ann

ONE

Living in the Moment

Carole Ann Drick

As I hung up the phone I felt an empty ache in my heart. My mother and I had been talking for over an hour and yet I wasn't satisfied. Something was different, incomplete. We had talked about our favorite topics - grandchildren, gardens, spirituality, ideas from reading. We always relished these talks for mutual nourishment and insight. Now it felt different. From where did this feeling come? Had it been there before and I just didn't recognize it?

I sat at the desk and gazed intently out the window into the backyard. The trees appeared the same; the flowers were blooming. Tears slowly filled my eyes. My mother, the woman who borne me, raised me, argued with me, encouraged me to seek higher ground, my mother was dying. Other girl friends' mothers had died. But, this was MY mother and she was dying.

The feeling opened to a physical ache in my heart that gradually deepened over the next four years. The daughter was becoming the witness, the friend, the confident, the wise one. Mother was imparting her last gifts to me.

After Dad's gentle death at home at 86, mother began a life alone after 52 years of his love and companionship. We talked often on the phone – the last washing of his clothes, figuring out the checkbook, the finances, taking out the trash, all the things Dad did became mother's full responsibility. She accepted this with a quiet resolution and the strength of her farm upbringing. Her Bachelor of Science in Home Economics from Penn State coupled with this upbringing resulted in a lifetime of searching for knowledge, understanding and truth. In these final years, this became even more apparent. Even today her quiet inner search for knowledge, understanding and truth is still evidenced in me, her daughter.

Visits Home

Living in the hill country of central Texas, I had realized about 5 years prior to that telephone call, the need to be closer to family so had moved to central Ohio – two hours from my youngest daughter, Janet, and five hours from mother in Buffalo, New York. My visits home became progressively more frequent moving from every 2-3 months to 6 weeks to 4 weeks to 2-3 weeks. The time with mother gradually expanded from 1 ½ days to 3 days and eventually to 4-5 days. With Janet's family being almost half way it was an easy trip to stop over night on the return trips and rejuvenate myself surrounded with the activity and love of her young family.

These visits were not always the easiest as mother was quite certain of what was best not only for herself but also for me. My adult life decisions did not always meet with her approval. She could be quite vocal in her opinions and declarations. These often left me feeling shattered until I realized that these were her opinions and had nothing to do with the underlying love and care she felt for me. As I focused on the underlying love and concern, I could hear her on a different level and it soon ceased to be threatening for me. At one point after a heated pronouncement mother said, "And you have no intention of following my direction, do you?" I smiled, felt the love rising within me, warming me and responded, "Probably not, mother. But, I deeply appreciate all the love and concern that is behind your thoughts." I had finally really heard what mother was saying - she was giving her gift of love in the only parental way she knew.

Quilting

After Dad's retirement mother began to quilt. Being a sewer all her life, this came easily. She immersed herself in quilting and soon my 2 daughters and I had quilts for every season of the year plus extras. Her initial "by the book" quilts soon gave way to an immense creativity flowing through her fingertips. The templates, the ideas for quilts flowed. Boxes and boxes of quilting material appeared. Plans for quilts, patterns, and designs - there were quilts in all stages of development. The formal dining room became the staging area with the large 8-chaired formal dining table the cutting, design and creation area.

On each of my visits home mother engaged me in the different stages of the quilting process. At one point I laughingly said, "Don't think for one moment I don't know what you are doing." She smiled what we often called her wise woman smile, laughed and said, "and one day this will all be yours, so pay attention!" This was one of the first breechings of her approaching death. It left a small lump of recognition in my throat.... ...always the teacher, always preparing and easing the way.

After her mini stroke when it became difficult to sew on the machine, mother focused her attention on design and cutting of squares, rectangles and even "last inch" postage size squares. Although no longer able to do the fine needlework, she shifted her attention to what she could do. When she was no longer able to thread needles, she asked whoever came to the house to thread dozens of needles so she could continue sewing and basting. Mother's attention shifted until one day she put large sign in bold black felt tip on the quilt rack in front of the dining room table, "QUILT SHOP is closed." The quilting tradition is being carried on with many plastic boxes of carefully sorted and labeled materials, patterns, and instructions now lining my basement walls. My inner creative center is becoming more easily accessible as my inner Stillness deepens though I often smile and wish I had paid more attention.

Prayer and Meditation Group

Mother had a weekly prayer and meditation group that had met for over 40 years. It started with over thirty women and was down to four – Margaret, Bobbi, Helen and Sara (mother). They were all in their 80's except Helen the baby by 10 years. As mother would say rather perturbed, "They just keep dying." Her prayer books were filled with dates, names and conditions for the focus of their prayer work. One could tell the state of the Union, of family and friends from her prayer books. My prayer books contain dates, names and written prayers for family, friends… "and the Union."

After Margaret "up and died on the group" there was no place to meet anymore. So the group of three continued to meet via the telephone with increasingly infrequent visits in between from Helen, the youngest. As part of our phone calls mother and I continued with the work of the prayer group.

Today my prayer group is spread across the country – Texas, California, Ohio, Kansas and Pennsylvania. We frequently talk, pray and stand in truth for each other thanks to "free" cell phone minutes, email and the infrequent hand written letter.

Driving

Mother was a good driver, fast but careful. Gradually she began to "allow" my brother and me to drive more and more of the time – but only in her car. When we were home, we were to drive her car to run errands and buy groceries. She began to "stock up" groceries at every visit so she didn't have to do so much "running around." Soon it became evident that we were doing the shopping for her. With the weekly prayer and meditation group ending her only other outing was the grocery store.

Mother never surrendered her driver's license. She just stopped driving. Her license expired without any talk of renewing it. She began to sit on the huge front porch more and more enjoying the neighborhood activity and people passing on the sidewalk. Her life was contracting to her home and its contents.

At one point near the end of her driving days, I arrived to find the spare set of keys on the kitchen table, the side door open and car gone. After unpacking and checking the food supply, walking the gardens and backyard, I was becoming worried. Calling her friends – all two of them, no they hadn't seen her. About 15 minutes later she came bursting into the kitchen with groceries and a "Well, there you are, I just couldn't wait for you – all the blueberries would have been picked over. I left the keys rather than a note... knew you'd figure it out with the car being gone." Mother didn't leave a note for fear someone else might read it and rob the house.

In the fall we went for long drives in the country on each of my visits. Reminiscing we would end up on her favorite country roads where the tree boughs reached over the road and the car was surrounded in a blaze of Western New York fall foliage. We also went out to a fish fry on Friday evenings. Even with her cane, then her walker, and finally for take out – Friday was fish fry night. How she relished her fish fry.

I relish the blaze of fall foliage, the taste of good fish fries and drive fast.

Cooking

Mother was an excellent cook. As a home economist, she not only taught cooking, she lived and enjoyed cooking. She had a drawer full of recipes that she had tried with notes on how to improve them. She cooked with what she had and taught her children that going to the store once a week was enough – just "plan out" your meals. Since she improvised and substituted ingredients, a dish was seldom the same two times in a row. She measured ingredients and then added more or less with a shrug of her shoulders and a "… that feels better."

At first mother insisted on doing all the cooking when I visited. I could talk with her and set the table, even wash the dishes and maybe put out the cold things. She began to talk about her cooking more and more as she prepared the food – always from scratch. I followed her lead and asked questions. Gradually I began to do more of the preparation and she began to do more of the auxiliary preparation. We talked about how I prepared the food; we compared notes and experimented.

As mother began to need rests in the afternoon, I often used that time to go to the grocery store. Mother was a comparison shopper and relished knowing where the best buys were located. She made her lists and compared and adjusted the lists until they met with her approval. One day as she laid down to rest she said wearily, "Well, I just didn't get to the shopping list. Now how will you know what to get?" She was holding the grocery ads in her hands and shaking her head. After a brief pause while helping her onto the bed and putting a blanket over her, I found myself saying, "Well, move over and we'll look at the ads together." The look of startled confusion on her face said it all, "What?" She started to move over. "Well, mother, who says that we can't look at the ads while you are lying down?" She laughed and said, "You're nuts." We laughed so hard as we lay on the bed looking at the food ads and talking. It was one of those real deep belly laugh times that relaxes and says that everything is just as it needs to be.

I continue to be a discriminative grocery shopper, cook using fresh whole foods rather than processed foods, shop once a week and improvise until "that feels better."

One day a phone call came. Her voice had an edge of bewilderment as she talked, "Carole." There was a long pause. "I just don't seem to be getting very much done these days. It seems like by the time I get dressed, eat breakfast, wash dishes, take my supplements that it's time to get lunch and that's how I'm spending my days. This isn't right.... and then I'm tired by 8:00 and fall into bed. I sleep all night and then do it again." Her life activities were contracting down to daily self care.

Meals on Wheels began 3 times a week with much dread and reluctance. By mother's standards the meals were awful. They certainly did not compare to either her or my cooking abilities. And she said so, often and repeatedly. Yet she also admitted that it was nice to have people come to see her and not have to fix her own meals all the time. Probably her worst problems with the food were the lack of a fresh salad and using canned vegetables.

Oh how she loved our visits, I'd bring organic meat and poultry plus fresh organic fruits and vegetables. She would eat with tears in her eyes and say, "I remember how good this tastes.... just like when I grew up on the farm.... This is so good and so healthy." To this day I continue to prepare organic foods and enjoy the deep rich tastes of all the foods.

Hygiene

Mother took great pride in her clothes and personal hygiene. As she began making adjustments in her daily routine, her personal hygiene changed. The clothes washer and dryer were located in the basement. As steps began to be a breathless experience she had me wash her clothes and hang them to dry – the dryer rusted out years ago. She and Dad just hung things and took them down when ever they remembered to get them. "NO, let's not fix the dryer," she would say as I would take the clothes to the basement to start the laundry. "This is just fine for now."

On my increasingly frequent visits I began changing the bed and starting a load of laundry. With my brother and I each coming about every 2-

3 weeks, the laundry got done. Gradually mother couldn't do any of the steps - either up to bed or down to the laundry. A bed and clothes were moved to the back family room. Mother began first floor living.

With only a half bath available mother spent time "bathing" at the sink. She'd say, "This is how I was bathed when I was little....oh, a fresh wash cloth on your face and arms is so refreshing."

Progressively mother had more difficulty taking care of her feet and lower legs. We started a "girls spa night" doing pedicures and foot massages. It became a favorite time of sharing and reminiscing.

In the last year there were fewer and fewer clothes to wash. Mother wore the same clothes often for 4 or 5 days. "And why not?" she would say. "I'm not getting them dirty and they don't smell.... Bathing everyday is greatly over rated.... My skin is so dry it needs a rest from all that water."

Constantly adapting to her changing situation, mother lived in the present moment adapting and figuring out what to do and how to do it. She was not afraid of living by herself. She turned the television on in late afternoon and it was on until 8:00 pm, her bedtime. I, personally, find myself living in the present moment, not by physical necessity rather from a place of deep realization. This is the only moment we have and to miss it through worry about the past or fear of the future is to miss life and the joy of living. On some level mother knew this also.

Falling

If mother had one recurrent fear – it was of falling. She began to talk about falling as her gait became increasingly unsteady. Finally, one day she called all breathless. She didn't bother to say hello, after all who else would be calling? "Well, it finally happened!" She paused and took a long slow breath. "I fell coming out of the bathroom. I just went right down in a heap and couldn't stop myself." "Oh, mother," I responded full of concern, "Are you all right? What did you do?" "Well, I just laid there a minute or two and moved everything to see if I was Okay." And I just thought, "Okay, Sara, here you are on the floor, now what are you going to do?" I rolled to my side and finally pushed myself up to all fours and doggie crawled to the kitchen chair and finally pulled myself up and sat down. Boy! I haven't worked that hard in a long time. Then I called you." "Well, how are you now, Mother?" "Well," she paused and then excitedly replied, "I know that I'm not going to break anything and I can get up so that's enough of that!" She raised her voice in determination at the end of the sentence. She continued with relief, "I don't need to worry about falling any more!" This topic of conversation was definitely over. Later we talked about getting an emergency call button to wear around her neck. She flatly refused to have anything to do with it.

Although mother fell several more times she always managed to fall on the softest carpet and the bruises, though distressing to her children, were minimal. Mother's self reliance was steadfast even in falling. This self-reliance of being in the moment and moving into solutions has been an ever-increasing gift to me.

Trip to California

Soon after my initial realization of mother's beginning decline and approaching death, she decided that we needed to fly to California to see Dr. Whitaker, a holistic physician, whose monthly newsletter she had been receiving for years. She felt that he could give her much more help than what she knew to do – and that was plenty. Her physician of many years "up and died on her and he was only 92!" His replacement was young, all textbook and didn't know the natural things that she had been using for over 40 years.

I arrived three days early to help her pack. Having been an extensive world traveler, I was surprised to see her suitcase with only a comb and toothbrush inside. "Oh, Carole, I just can't seem to remember what to pack. I start and then get so tired." So we packed together taking more than half a day with much reminiscing about her and Dad's international travels.

On the December morning of our departure the six inches of new snow was met with concerns about getting to the airport on time. The neighbor was already out, shoveled the driveway and at the front door 10 minutes early. Excited and slightly flustered with the attention, Mother managed to walk down the front steps with her cane and get into the car. The excitement lasted until we arrived at the airport. As we helped her out of the car her eyes widened and she gasped, "Oh, Carole, I don't remember…. It all feels so strange. Stay close to me." Refusing a wheelchair we checked baggage at curbside and proceeded into the terminal. Travel was easier in those days without the maze of lines and checkpoints. Being early on a Sunday there were few fellow travelers. As we started toward the gate her steps became slower. We stopped to look out the huge floor to ceiling airport windows. The steps became even slower. "It's a lot further than I remembered. I can't make it." She sat down at the next available seat, sighing and shaking her head. We looked around at the people passing by. "Oh, mother, what you need is an airport limo and we are in luck. Look!" Next to where she had sat down was an empty wheelchair. "Redeemed!!!" she laughed.

Once seated on the plane mother said with a sigh, "Of course you know this is why I asked you along – to be my eyes, ears and legs." Arriving at John Wayne International Airport, CA mother accepted the offered wheelchair.

For the next seven days we were part of a group of seventeen who were evaluated and put on both a natural treatment regime and "good balanced meals" which delighted mother not to mention all the attention for being the oldest attendee. She needed repeated cues to know which way to turn to reach the elevators, our room, the dining area and the meeting area. Her ability to remember people's names and her conversation skills were excellent. She was in her element.

On the flight home she said, "You know, I couldn't have done this without you. I didn't realize how contracted I am in the house." Later she reflected, "So we spent all this money to find out what you have been telling me and I've felt all along.... I'm fine. My heart is enlarged but it is strong."

"Yes, Mother, you got it."

This trip satisfied mother in knowing she was physically Okay. In fact she clung to this no matter what any physician said. For the rest of her life her response was, "I am fine." Talk about stubbornness or maybe it was truth coming through. Mother WAS fine. For me the trip reaffirmed the accuracy of the intuitive health counseling and testing that I had been doing with her. Even more important, "I am fine" - the real me, the eternal me is fine no matter what anyone says or anything that happens to the body.

Hospitalization

The phone call came about 4:00 pm. The hospital called saying my brother had given permission for mother's admission, as they couldn't contact me. Mother had slipped between the bed and the wall and couldn't get out. The Meals on Wheels volunteers found her and called the paramedics.

Talking with mother she said she was shaken with all the excitement but fine. Yes, I was on my way and would call her when I got into town. I would see her in the hospital in the morning. I spent a quick half hour packing then started the five hour drive to Buffalo, New York.

We spent the next several days talking while mother was "being observed." She decided that was the lingo for "taking your money and doing nothing."

On the second day mother said, "Carole, something is happening." She paused as I looked at her and waited. "I'm loosing time. I start combing my hair and the next thing I know another program has started on the television. If my roommate didn't have the television on all the time I never would have known."

We sat in silence then I said, "What... what do you think it is?"

Mother turned and looked deep into my eyes. "I feel like I'm having mini strokes."

"Really?" I responded with concern. "What shall we do about this?"

"Nothing and you aren't to do anything either. Just let nature take its course."

My entire nurse training and years of working with patients had not prepared me for this response. My heart stopped as I swallowed hard, "Oh, Mother, are you sure?"

"Yes, my dear, it's time. It's been time for a while. I miss Dad. It's been a good life. I'm ready," She patted my hand,

"You are Okay - better than Okay."

My eyes filled with tears as I nodded in agreement. We sat in silence holding hands and drinking in each other with our eyes. I heard the words yet sat in disbelief that this was happening. Breathing deeply I smiled and gazed deeply into my mother's eyes – so peaceful, so understanding.

The next morning the doctor decided mother needed rehabilitation to strengthen her legs and get her moving better. Mother insisted that I go home to Ohio and get things prepared. She was fine. I left with a heavy heart and traveled the five hours home.

I called her everyday and we talked and shared and reminisced. About five days later during an especially high energy call, her voice changed and she said in a gentle yet serious tone, "Carole, I feel that I won't be coming home... and it's fine. Everything is being taken care of."

The day before mother was to be transferred to the rehabilitation center the neighbor called. Mother had a stroke during the early morning hours and they thought she would come out of it fine. Calling the nurses' station, the report I received was different. Her nurse with fourteen years of experience felt it was much more serious than the physician thought. Asking the nurse to describe what she saw, I could hear my mother's voice inside me saying, "It's Okay. It's time." Asking if mother could respond the nurse said she could by nodding but her eyes were closed. I asked her to hold the phone to mother's ear and let me pray with her. The nurse needed only to say in a loud voice that she was nodding yes or no.

"Mother, this is Carole Ann. It's time now to go deep within, into that beautiful warm light and stay there. You are so loved and you will be missed, and yes, it is Okay.... Keep going into the light.... There you are safe and whole and perfect.... We will take care of the physical.... Jay loves you.... I love you.... We all love you.... Just keep going home...."

I heard the nurse saying in a loud voice, "She is nodding yes." I prayed with Mother until I felt the full crown energy flood through our bodies. I knew that everything was in Divine Order.

Hanging up the phone I called my brother in Michigan, packed my bags and started the long trip to Buffalo. I called the hospital when I arrived. The nurse reported that after I had talked with mother she had become unresponsive. I called my oldest daughter, Kimberly, the nurse in Nashville, Tennessee. Without hesitation she said, "I'm on my way." My brother arrived later in the day.

On the way to the hospital I explained to my brother that mother was gone, but her body was still functioning – like going on vacation and leaving the lights on in the house – there's no one home.

We spent most of the next day with mother. Talking, laughing and reminiscing about our growing up. My brother was temporarily hopeful when he felt one of mother's occasional involuntary hand muscle contractions as the body was relaxing and releasing. At one point mother's right arm involuntarily rose and was suspended in mid air. We both stopped in mid sentence and stared. Jay then laughed and said, "It's Okay, Mom, you don't have to raise your hand, just jump in." We laughed as I said "Here let me put your arm in a more comfortable position" as I gently lowered it to her side. We moved mother to a hospice bed in the hospital and made her comfortable. When we left we both said our good byes, our thank you's for a wonderful life together, and how much we loved her.

Jay needed to return to Michigan. I planned to stay. Kimberly arrived late the next afternoon after driving 16 hours straight. Rather than sleeping she gave me a long deep hug and said, "Let's go see grandmother." Kimberly took in one of mother's favorite quilts and a small radio to play classical music.

That evening Kimberly came over to me, put her arms around me and said, "Mom, I want you to go home and do what you do best – pray. Let me take care of grandmother. It's my last gift to her. Please, mom, let me do this."

With tears streaming down our faces we held each other, cried and nodded agreement. We both slept well that night. In the morning I left for Ohio and Kimberly went to the hospital. She called each day for the next three days. I spent the days in deep prayer and meditation in a place I call "deep space nine." On the fourth day I received an early morning call about 6:45 am. "Mom, Grandmother just died. She had been gasping all night and I just crawled in bed with her and put my arms around her and said softly in her ear, "Oh, Grandmother, you have been working so hard all night to breathe. It's daylight now and you don't have to work any harder. It's Okay. You are fine." And, MOM, she took three easier breaths and left." The tears in our eyes and the sadness in our hearts filled the empty silence that followed.

Leaving my mother as she was leaving this physical plane is probably one of the most difficult things I have ever done… allowing my daughter to give her gift of nursing care and Kimberly allowing me to give my gift of prayer. Who could ask for anything more? The gifts of love and depth of caring had come full circle.

In the ensuing days I found myself in a place of deep Inner Peace and when the feelings of sadness and loss did come they were surrounded with an Inner Peace and a feeling of comfort that everything is really just as it needs to be. It was a feeling of deepening contentment and abiding in awareness with each day.

Postscript

Two and a half years later the estate is settled, the physical remembrances distributed to family and friends. I am constantly amazed at the power and strength that is growing in me. The sadness of physical loss has turned into cherishing memories and discovering the unexpected gifts that mother is still giving to me – resourcefulness, going within, creative meals, not putting my hands at the top of the steering wheel – "that's how old ladies drive. I might be little and I might be old but I don't drive like that." Knowing that I'm Okay – better than Okay.

Although I desperately wanted my mother's verbal approval for most of my life, I have discovered that she was continually giving it to me as she entrusted me more and more with her care and finally her last requests. I am realizing, no I am living more in the moment, cherishing my grandchildren – on my belly playing on the floor with them, laughing a good belly laugh, stopping to enjoy the sunsets, living a life of integrity, allowing love to rise from deep stillness, and knowing that this moment is just as it needs to be.

Being in the present moment by dying to/ releasing the last moment has set me free to enjoy life as it presents itself, to be more spontaneous and give thanks for each situation, each person, each moment of life. I continue to marvel at how the breath starts in the formless, fills my lungs and then returns to the formless.... how everything returns to the formless, the unmanifested, everything.

TWO

She is Now Wherever We Are

Barbara Dossey

As I sat and held Mother's face in my hands almost a year ago—bearing witness to her journey between two worlds—I was profoundly struck by how life changes in a flash. Reflecting on my deep relationship with Mom all of my life, the words that a friend sent to me pop into my mind: "She whom we love and lose is no longer where she was before. She is now wherever we are." Although my meditation practice, my work in holistic nursing, my compassionate care of the dying, and my/our personal healing rituals assisted us in Mom's transition, I found that nothing really prepares us completely for the death of a loved one.

Before I began to write about Mom today, I engaged in several healing rituals to bring me into this moment to share Mom's story and the gifts she gave me in her dying. These included looking at Mom's most recent church picture in her pretty light-blue spring suit, and my favorite picture of Mother (5'1") and Daddy (6'4") just before he died nine years ago. I also opened my "Mother" computer file and looked at the digital photos my sister made of Mom's last 50 hours, and listened to her voice recording from her phone message recorder that she never changed over 35 years. Yes, tears still come. I miss her so and am aware of talking to her all the time, but not by phone.

December 2004 holidays were very special because Mom, age 86, had been very sick in the fall. She had regained her strength and confidence, and was ready to play bridge and drive again. She had been to several Christmas parties and was so delighted to be visiting her friends and wearing her pretty clothes and jewelry, rather than experiencing their visits to her in her robe at home. In early December, my sister and I had decorated Mom's front porch while she gave us a few suggestions. To our pleasant surprise, it won a Christmas door prize at her retirement village. On the evening of December 25, we had a lovely Christmas dinner and a restful Christmas afternoon.

The day after Christmas, around 8:00 a.m., Mom had a mild transient ischemic attack (TIA). She completely recovered and had a very engaged day with us, laughing, relaxing, working her crossword puzzles and reading. When I asked her if she wanted to discuss her TIA, she smiled and said "No thank you. I am very aware of what happened since many of my friends have experienced them." Some of these friends were at her retirement village or in her church and had recovered, while others had had debilitating strokes, were in wheelchairs, couldn't speak or care for themselves, or had died.

When my sister and I asked her how she felt about having a TIA, she laughed and said, "Well, my brain is getting a little less confused, and it simply is just what happened. Thank heavens I'm now here, alert, talking, walking and moving!"

There was a palpable Presence that radiated from Mom all day that was extraordinary. She and the family knew that an unusual event had occurred. With an "engaged watching," Mom seemed to track all of us in our activities or conversations in a different way. My sister and I commented on this to each other; we also discussed with her our experience of her engaged watching. Mom's response to us was not verbal; she just gave us her adorable, wide smile in which her eyes would always disappear. The rest of the day she looked at us as if she knew that her time with us was coming to an end.

My knowing at this time was that this was very possible because it is not usual for a stroke to follow a TIA. But most of all there seem to be an Inner Wisdom coming forth.

Our delicious dinner and lively conversations captured us around the dinner table until 10:30p.m. at which time I looked at Mom, saw that she looked really tired, and suggested she go to bed. She said she was very tired indeed, and promptly got up, walked to her bedroom, and got in bed—easily done, since she already had on her gown. My sister sensed that something was wrong as Mom always kissed each of us goodnight before retiring. Tonight Mom had neglected to do this. My sister went to Mom's room to indeed find that she was confused, but this confusion passed quickly. A short time later, before leaving for the evening, my brother, sister, brother-in-law, niece, and nephew kissed Mom goodnight before she drifted to sleep.

Thirty minutes later, Mom awoke and was confused. Larry, my husband and I went to her bedroom. Her last words to us were "take me home." We told her that she was at home, and if by chance she saw another place called home she should feel free to go there. Because she was confused, I told Larry that I was going to stay with her until she went back to sleep, and I climbed into her bed. I had done this so many times, either to chat or watch a television movie with her. I was aware that this could be my last time to be with her and felt a deep sense of this being a sacred space and time.

Since Mom was resting on her back, I lay on my right side and rested my hand on the center of her chest, at which point she immediately placed both of her hands on my hand. I gently turned my hand and grasped hers, and then we both drifted to sleep. Mom had a massive stroke at 2:05 the next morning, December 27. She became diaphoretic, which woke me up as my hand still was on her chest. Turning on the light, I saw that Mom's eyes were deviated to one side and that she was unresponsive. I knew that the most important think was just to be with her in these precious moments. I never imagined that I would be with her in this time between two worlds. This experience of "being with" remains beyond words. My tears were joyful and I was conscious of releasing her in this physical life form. It was so clear to me that my meditation practice of releasing attachment to the physical body had become a part of my beingness.

About 30 minutes later, Larry awoke and came to Mom's room to check on us. Since Mom had signed her Living Will, we honored her wishes and provided comfort care, love, and prayers in her home for the next two days. We intuitively knew that this was the right thing to do. The knowingness that was coming forward was that this was a sacred journey with Mom.

Although Mom was unresponsive, her blood pressure and heartbeat were strong. The gift of Larry's presence, as I talked and rehearsed this last day was that Presence is what serves us in healing the wounds of loss and grief. My experience as a nurse, and Larry's as an internist, prepared us for what lay ahead. I waited till 7:00 a.m. to call the family to tell them about Mom. Together, my sister and I made a "to do" list and set in motion immediate tasks and people to contact. Mom's doctor placed her on hospice; within a few hours the hospice nurse had helped us create the flow of comfort-care procedures and medication for Mom. The family engaged in healing rituals such as bathing Mom, reading her favorite Bible verses, and sitting quietly with her. This was a time of moving with intention in slow motion; there was no rushing. We made sure we included Mom's two caregivers and her young sisters who had attended her since late September. Throughout the day we sat with Mom, either together or alone for extended periods. For all of us to be present in these last hours was utterly sacred. Beyond words we could feel this sacredness deepen as the veil between the physical world and the spiritual world became very thin.

Mom made her transition with elegance, grace, and gentleness on December 30 at 2:58 a.m. Several hours prior, we gave her a final bath, washed and set her hair, painted her nails with pale, pink polish, and placed her favorite pink lipstick on her, and then dressed her in a beige gown. It was an honoring of her physical body and preparation for the soul's journey home. All of my life's work in holistic nursing and compassionate care of the dying seemed to be for this moment.

Because Mom had been so sick in the fall, she knew that death was near. During this period she had discussed details about all of her affairs with both my sister and me. She had shown me the specific pink gown she was to be buried in. She had made known to me the details of all of her affairs, including names and phone numbers, her attorney files, where her will could be found, her banking and lockbox information, her burial insurance policy, and details about her burial plot, casket and service. She had even written her obituary, had listed the pallbearers and their phone numbers, and had talked to her minister and provided him statements for her funeral service that would celebrate her life. A wonderful surprise was our discovery of a 12-page autobiography, "The Road to Success," that she had written and stored with all her papers. She also had written each of her children a personal letter in her gorgeous handwriting. Such gifts! What empowerment, what preparation. She had consciously finished her earthly business and was transferring the responsibility of the family legacy to us. It was at this point that I became aware of being the oldest in my family in a new way. Yes, I have always acted like the first born, but now it felt different. To cherish these last sacred hours, we stayed with her until late morning before we called hospice to release her to the funeral home. The experience was like floating in space and time. My inner awareness was that when we have done some previous work on releasing a loved one prior to death, as well as our own work of releasing attachment each day, then when death comes it can be a gentle and subtle shift in conscious awareness, nothing more, nothing less.

The beautiful service and burial were on January 3, 2005. Prior to closing Mom's rose bronze gold-brushed silver casket we kissed her good-bye for the last time on this physical plane. I experienced her deep love for all of us. It felt like she was pleased with all of us, and what we had done in these last hours. Mom had on her favorite, pink-lace gown, her rose-beige pashmina shawl around her shoulders, her pink lipstick. My sister and I artistically connected family pictures with yellow, pink and beige ribbons with silk roses attached. Daddy's favorite putter, golf glove, golf ball were tucked by her side to send her on her way. Mom's preparation for her journey to the other world was complete.

The service was a celebration journey that unfolded in such a lovely way. Our precious mother had been so considerate of all of us until the end. It was so obvious that before her stroke, Mom was preparing this moment ahead of time as was evidenced with the physical preparations. Yet even more, in her deep love and her final caring for the family in these preparations, she had smoothed the time for us so we could be in the moment and allow everything to unfold gently and easily. Her kindness and attention to details throughout her life is part of the sense of continuation of her spirit with me at all times.

Mom's profound gifts to me in her transition were a deeper understanding of not-knowing, bearing witness, and healing of self and others. Not-knowing is allowing the mind to move beyond the attachment to fixed ideas about self or others. It is being able to be comfortable with the present moment however it presents itself. Bearing witness means that we are present for the suffering of self and others and are not trying to fix anything. It reminds us to be fully present for what is, in our lives and the world. It includes the ability to tap our human capacity, to step aside and listen to our inner voice, and to experience our thoughts, feelings, and images without attachment. Going to the core of deep listening and inner wisdom can break the ego attachment to our human form, as all of us move toward our own death moment. Healing is our lifelong journey into wholeness. It asks us to make a whole tapestry of all the pieces of our lives, to include everything, reject nothing.

Our journey is truly to understand that there are no boundaries between physical life, the form, and death of the form. Both are complementary dimensions of the same unified experience. Death is always present everywhere in life. Nothing last forever. To experience one is simultaneously to experience the other. I am more aware each day of accepting the daily little deaths such as releasing fears, anxieties, and disappointments so that these can prepare me for my own physical death moment.

Mom's gifts in her dying have helped me more fully understand how true healing includes dying in peace, and releasing one's attachment to the physical body. It is learning to let our body-mind-spirit be open to the only true healing, the healing that comes from within. This is an interesting paradox that can appear in many ways throughout our lives. Although this healing awareness may appear at first to be rare, it is a very ordinary and a very natural event available to us at all times. As we practice living in peace, we enter a healing state where answers to our questions about the complementary nature of living and dying are revealed to us. The insight we gain adds to our own inner wisdom and strength.

As I shared Mom's journey with a friend, she reminded me that this was a rite of passage, a changing of the guard in which I was now the eldest member of my family. I have accepted the passage of the "talking stick" to me from Mother. I am now the elder, the carrier of the family traditions. I honor this sacred experience. I must continue my meditation practices to be in this present moment so that when my death moment comes, I will have the grace and dignity to leave on my own terms as Mom did, and to pass my responsibilities to the next elder in line.

Accepting the truth of physical death is how I am able to begin to go beyond fear and fully engage my life. This offers me a way to question what I am doing at this very moment, and to recognize what is important in preparing for my dying and the experience of death itself.

Mom has taught me in her passing that it is not morbid to dwell on one's death. Doing so is, in a sense, a kind of preventive medicine - not that we can eliminate death, but that we can transcend the suffering and horror that our culture associates with it. This view is captured in a Zen saying, "If you die before you die, then when you die you will not die."

As I practice being in the moment, I can arouse awareness in relation to how I am living my life. What am I doing now to deepen my experience? How am I working with my own fear and suffering, and that of others? What am I doing now to prepare for dying and for death? What am I doing, then, to prepare not only for liberation at the moment of death, but also for liberation at this moment?

Physical life involves challenges that include pain and suffering. Pain is physical and/or emotional discomfort; suffering is the story that develops around our pain. When I awaken to the realization that pain and suffering are part of being human, I am more able to discover the wisdom and compassion that these experiences can convey. Knowing that pain and suffering exist, I can try to discover the cause of my suffering, and understand that I can bring an end to suffering through a path that enables me to become free of it.

My journey with Mom also deepened my experience around the four qualities of compassionate care. *Loving kindness* is an open, gentle, and caring state of presence with self and others. *Compassion* is feeling others' or one's own suffering. *Sympathetic joy* is the profound elation we experience as we regard the well-being of others and ourselves. *Equanimity*, the perfect partner of compassion, is the stability of mind that allows us to be present with an open heart, no matter how wonderful, beneficial, or difficult the conditions or experiences may be. When our worldview makes room for the truth of impermanence, the interconnectedness of phenomena, and the possibility of freedom from suffering, we are better able to face and work with suffering and loss. Life is impermanent, but it is precisely because of impermanence that we value life.

My grieving process has increased my awareness of the importance of healing rituals, both private and those shared with my family and friends. Often, out of nowhere, a memory, a song, or a daily household task like cleaning, washing dishes, doing the laundry, or preparing a meal evokes a sense of loss that goes to my core, causing pain so intense it seems it will never heal. I have learned that I can stay in that experience only so long before love and joy fill my heart again. The wisdom is to let pain in and to stay open to it, to go through and not around it, knowing that what emerges from the pain may be a new level of healing.

It is impossible for me to stop thinking about Mom. Her presence is continual, and reminds me of a poem that I often read or recite, by Henry Scott Holland (1847–1918), the Canon of St. Paul's Cathedral, London:

Death is nothing at all. I have only slipped away into the next room. I am I, and you are you. Whatever we were to each other, that we still are. Call me by my old familiar name, speak to me in the easy way which you always used. Put no difference in your tone, wear no forced air of solemnity or sorrow. Laugh as we always laughed at the little jokes we enjoyed together. Pray, smile, think of me, pray for me. Let my name be ever the household word that it always was, let it be spoken without affect, without the trace of a shadow on it. Life means all that it ever meant. It is the same as it ever was; there is unbroken continuity. Why should I be out of mind because I am out of sight? I am waiting for you, for an interval, somewhere very near, just around the corner. All is well.

THREE

Another Time and Another Place

Enberdine Voute-Hummes

It's been twenty years since my mother's death. She was 95 and I was 2 months short of 60. It was another time and another place. The years have a way of distancing memories, forgetting some and enhancing others.

I grew up in the Netherlands many years ago. Death was considered part of living – a deeply felt experience happening in the course of every day life. It was not hidden or a taboo subject but it was openly and even lovingly talked about. When a death occurred it was experienced as one of the celebrated milestones of life – as birth, marriage, baptisms were the joyful occasions. It was a gathering of family and friends reminiscing and reflecting upon life together and individually.

When my mother died I lived far away from her in America. My brother made it possible for me to fly to Holland to see her, but she could not communicate any more. My older brother and I stayed with her in her room. We read old correspondence – letters we wrote about our lives – and remembered both our parents' interest in our daily happenings within and outside of our families. Even though separated by so many miles, they were part of the children's activities and accomplishments through letters and even visits. After a week I sadly had to fly back to my family in America and could not stay any longer at Mother's bedside. My sister-in-law and Mother were very close. She was ill also. I believe she was still waiting for me as well to come and say goodbye.

Mother died October 10,1984 at age 95 and as the season around us, her dying inspired a sense of fulfillment, accomplishment and well-deserved rest. I was not able to be there. Since then I have gradually come to realize that life is a gift manifested in the reality of each person, making us all part of the eternal cycle of energy. Within this span of time we strive for harmony within oneself and with others – a continuing challenge to cope and to make decisions. Mother lived her life well using the tools and talents allotted her and earned her rest.

While alive she gave of herself – all she had to give and then she was gone. Her legacy stayed. With my own aging comes a deeper understanding of Mother's struggle to overcome her problems of mental instability and health issues. I appreciate her example of welcoming each new day as an opportunity to learn. She passed on the values of endurance and patience. Often we heard her quote "all comes as it has to be, though differently from how you think it shall be."

Mother did not have an easy life. Born in 1899 and raised in Berlin in an aristocratic old family, she was ill prepared to have to earn money for her family after her father died. He had lost his fortune co-signing for a friend in a deal that went sour. My grandmother had no skills – my uncle was too young yet to work. We rarely talked about my mother's youth and facts are sketchy. She lived in Berlin during World War I with its hard times and famine. Then in 1923 on a vacation in the Harz Mountains, she met my father – a romantic story. Only weeks later she came to the Netherlands to live with my father's family till her marriage. The family with three sisters did not exactly welcome her with open arms. Mother learned the language and the Dutch ways of doing things – even riding a bicycle.

Unfortunately, Mother was plagued by depressions and had a nervous breakdown. She even tried to commit suicide while pregnant with me the youngest of three children. Therefore necessarily much of her energy was spent on herself to learn to cope and function in order to meet the demands made on her.

When I was four, my grandmother took quite ill. She came to stay with us so we could care for her. I remember my mother coming into the garden, where I played with water and a green enamel pail, to tell me that she could not care for both Oma and me. Therefore, I was to go to school to live. I felt not wanted, but with a typical child naiveté accepted the decision without questioning the reason. That is when I left home and had to stand on my own little legs. I often think that is when I had to take on adult responsibility.

Mother gave all she had to give, which was maybe less and different than we kids wished. Mother had a very active mind. She read many books and sometimes when I would like to tell her about my experiences in school or about my time with my best friend there was little reaction or indication that she even heard anything of my story. It seemed as if my mother's face looked like the cover of a book, as she did not look up from her reading. Though she was always present at high times in my life, such as Girl Scout ceremonies, I was independent in my activities and daily doings, responsible for my schoolwork and chores – responsible in my own little world. I did not question this - "that's just the way it is.

What I have received and learned

Teaching is often giving an example. Mother courageously dealt with her handicap of depressions and physical illness of migraines.

Mother was an avid reader. She instilled the importance of being interested in everything – whether it was literature, history, science or social concerns. She studied philosophy at age 90! I must suppose that books offered her insight and wisdom that supported her in her decision making. Her reading exposed her to the joy of life as well. As she read a great variety of literature she developed an open-mindedness and acceptance of different views, allowing, no doubt, a certain freedom of thinking – an independence and inner strength.

I also like to read and start the day with a book before the daily busy hours rob me of the time.

Literature about people in settings of other times in history and other places are my favorites. To glean the similarity of problems and psychological make-up of the characters and societies, as well as the differences of attitude and outlook on life, and to learn from this through reflection upon it, is for me learning that can be practiced in my own life.

Folkart is my passion – an expression of inner feelings and often religious needs. It is an incredible down-to-earth psychology and philosophy in expression. Just as Mother taught me crafts as a form of expression, I can transfer Folkart learning into realities through weaving loom, needles and paintbrushes.

Mother coped with difficulties and danger. During WWII my older brother was hidden from the Germans to avoid being sent to the factories there. My younger brother, though too young yet, was almost hauled off to Germany. He was rescued in the nick of time by pulling him off a truck by my father, who had been warned of the situation via the community grapevine. My family was involved with the underground, harboring wanted men and Jews – men who stood on the German "wanted list" and had to sleep at a different address every night in an attempt to escape discovery and being sent to the concentration camps. One night when we were a few minutes late returning home and when the full moon shone brightly, our guest did not dare stay longer outside waiting and went to the next address. Someone, however, had seen him and the next day our house was surrounded by German soldiers who exercised a razzia – a search through the house.

Had they found him or my brother who was hidden or anything else that we were not allowed to have such as the radio, more than two blankets per bed, stored food, we would all have been hauled off to the concentration camps. Courageously my parents put their very existence and lives on the line, time and again. What was morally right was more important than the risk to one's own welfare.

Mother knew her limitations and needed plenty of sleep. Her daily nap between 1:00 and 3:00 was sacred – nobody would disturb her. A sign on the door kept possible visitors from ringing the bell. Her headache powders - those old-fashioned ones, the loose powder folded in a parchment paper and delivered in a flowered pharmacy box, were constant companions on her bedside table. Every morning, however, no matter how she felt she would preside over the breakfast table and send the family on their way to work or school.

Mother was a good organizer and socially aware. She taught by example to get involved – doing instead of talking. She organized concerts at home to benefit the underground during the war. She founded a Girl Scout troop illegally under the Germans and later served as District Commissioner. She led fundraiser – town fairs, dance performances with the princesses, even Christmas bazaars.

Mother's moral character lives on in me as I follow in her footsteps being involved in different endeavors. For many years I served in church in various capacities – led an International Girl Scout troop bridging the programs of the U.S.A, Britain and Germany, organized fundraisers, brought people together for tea or knitting or exchanging thoughts and experiences – just reaching out.

Though religion and church had no important place in our lives, mother had great faith and spirituality. She passed on to us this open-mindedness to all beliefs. My older brother even became a minister and professor of religion! Humans are gifted with the privilege of thinking and choosing their paths of belief. Many roads can lead to the same end at which one reaches a higher plateau of awareness and tolerance of others. Mother showed us the value of studying other ways of living, thinking and believing. She showed us how to be free to find one's own conviction while respecting others.

Mother also taught the meaning of celebrating on special occasions as well as in daily life. Dinner hour was the day's focus. Table manors were taught as a family inheritance of respect. At feast meals the special crystal compotes sparkled and the wine was served with almost ceremony. As the only girl in the household, Mother taught me the importance of these gestures as a sense of continuation of family.

Tradition was an important part of our lives. Her heritage was continued and Dutch customs added. Especially at Christmas time we learned about her German customs. The Christmas tree was decorated with the candleholders of her youth. The story was told of the importance of the lighting of the candles for the first time on Christmas Eve. The caroling and reading stories were continued as a form of continuance. An evening of meaningful celebration was always a part of Christmas. Mother never spoke German with us, but for every occasion or happening she would quote something in her native language. We would grow up familiar with the sounds and the realization that thoughts can be expressed in different words.

An intense sense of continuation – a flow from generation to generation – was instilled in us. This sense of continuation, this gift of flow continues today as I remember her ways and the sayings as I am passing them on to my children. They all went to their first day of school with their "Zuckertuete" – a cone shaped container full of candy to sweeten the seriousness of starting life in the outside world.

Then and Now

At the time of my mother's death my feelings and thoughts embraced gratefulness. Although the gratefulness has increased over these 20 years it has also enlarged into an ever-increasing depth of knowing and being. I was grateful for mother's doing to her utmost ability. I think she grew to realize her talents and limitation – to use them wisely and so found her way to cope with all that came towards her. In spite of hurdles she did not give up.

I was grateful for learning independence, courage, and a continuing interest in all aspects of life, spirituality and tradition. This has expanded into seeing the larger picture of things and not getting caught up in the minutia. I find myself still getting exasperated at times but it is easier to step back and get perspective.

Finally, I was grateful to learn a deeper awareness of life as part of a larger existence from generation to generation with faith in an unknown purpose. This continuity of life continues to be expressing not only from generation to generation but into eternity. It's both a physical continuity and a spiritual continuity. My faith is enlarging with each passing day knowing that everything is part of this purpose. I might not know or completely understand, but I do know that I play a part in moving this purpose forward. The cyclical flow of seasons, of life spans, of the universe – all inspire the acceptance of this continuity and the realization of being a part of it. This is an acceptance expressed spiritually as well as in the gestures of day-to-day life. The purpose need not be known to follow an innate guideline to achieve some harmony in the flow of existence and to experience life's energy itself.

Even though we were not "close", Mother, I thank you for your teachings through example. Thank you for living your life the way you did. Your gifts, your teachings, the continuity of life all are alive and growing in your grandchildren and in me.

FOUR

Free Will, Positive Attitude and Life

Elizabeth Bachofer

Looking back, Mom had ill health for years and years. The first big event was going into diabetic shock in the mid-1970s… a big scary event for this 11 year old. She felt lucky to have it discovered and treatment started. Trouble was, since she didn't feel bad, she tended to ignore the disease. She didn't mind the three times a day insulin shots; she just didn't want to change her behavior. She ate and drank whatever struck her fancy. The only noticeable change was switching from regular soda pop to sugar free soda pop. Exercise was brief and not consistent. As much as we would beg her, she did what she pleased. And she would be extremely moody when we would beg/plead with her to do the things the doctor recommended for her health. So eventually we stopped talking to her about her eating and exercise.

Mom had a tremendous laugh, and was always the life of the party. Now my father traveled out of town Monday-Thursday each week so mother had us three girls to manage completely while he was gone.

I am the oldest. She enrolled us in events for kids at the catholic college from which she had graduated. If there was a concert in the park or the municipal auditorium we went. She volunteered with meals on wheels, the local summer festival, anything new and exciting we went and enjoyed and participated. It was great fun. She enjoyed life to the fullest, no reservations. It was a great attitude. One that I embrace as best I can.

The bedeviling question is how can someone so filled with life, brimming with a thirst to drink it all in, not choose life affirming health decisions? Is it the immediacy of pleasure that propelled her addiction to food?

I remember how much she liked being in the hospital. They brought food; she could lie around and watch television - kind of being pampered. She had many health crises; each seemed to progressively be more dramatic and serious. Mom had uterine cancer in the early 1980s and a heart attack in the early 1990s. By the mid 1990s she couldn't walk far because of heart troubles but she hid it well. On vacations she could hang out on the beach and allow everyone else to explore the area. She professed to be comfortable and doing exactly what she wanted to do.

Much is written about having a positive mental attitude. She had that to the extreme. Once while in the hospital with a life threatening blood clot in her leg, her brother visited her and asked how she was doing. She responded in her cheery way that everything was fine, and really meant it. Later that day I heard my Uncle say my mom was being her usual self, acting like an ostrich with its head in the sand. In essence, ignoring the problem. That was exactly the issue. She had speedy recoveries, but never could deal with the underlying issue causing the ill health. But to be fair, in that moment, when he asked, she was fine. What else are you going to do? Lie there and stress out? That doesn't aid in recovery. A little self-examination may have been what he was looking for when he asked that question, and didn't see any occurring.

What bugs me about this is my knowing that with prayer and the use of positive thought and action, many of her trips to the hospital could have been avoided or at least minimized. She used the principles of prayer and positive thought but did not implement the second part of the formula. Treat and move your feet. Speak the truth and then move from that truth. These are prayer sayings. We have to implement the inspiration and be open to the direction and help we receive. This includes both medical and intuitive knowledge of proper food consumption and exercise.

To her credit, Mom's employment choices took her on the road looking for help. She started as an elementary teacher, then a social worker, athletic secretary, weight loss clinic secretary, and finally a medical office secretary. I sometimes think she was looking for answers but none could help her or she couldn't implement the help they offered. For me at that point, surrender to God is the only answer. Mom was Catholic through and through, yet she never found help in implementing self-discipline. Her motto seemed to be - enjoy the moment; live the moment; tomorrow be damned!

I struggle with this myself, wanting certain results without disciplining my appetites. I've heard the concepts of "being in integrity with yourself," along with "honoring your inner knowingness" and "listen to your inner intelligence."

I undertook a study of healing and broke away from my family. It wasn't a rejection of them as much as a searching for another way of living. Through this study I learned better ways to use positive thinking, and implementing food choices. I found freedom from lifelong allergies. For as long as I can remember, each time I woke up I sneezed three times. What freedom it is to be free from that! I discovered wheat and dairy caused those symptoms—my favorite food groups. I love pizza, cereal with milk, grilled cheese sandwiches. As I stopped consuming diet soda the gray fog that would seem to descend around my mental states cleared away. Not consuming my favorite foods was very challenging. But I found such relief that it propelled me into making one good choice after another.

The last few years I have slipped back into poor food choices. In examining the choices my mother made, I am sad to see myself lapsing into laziness—or more accurately—unconscious living. I really don't need nor want a major health challenge to slap me awake. Reviewing my Mom's declining health has really helped me to wake up and begin to make better decisions about my food choices and my life.

Now, part of this story is that the last seven years of my mom's life she was on a ventilator, unable to talk, unable to dress herself, unable to cook, unable to be left unattended for more than a minute. Really. This is not an overstatement. When we, as a family, made the decision to bring her home from the hospital, the medical staff told us she probably wouldn't last a year. Well, she lived for seven. And, it was not only a major commitment, but also life altering for each of us. During those years I struggled with my commitment, and the stress it put on my life.

Neale Donald Walcsh's book *Home with God* has given me a lot more insight about those seven years. Some things I read brought me to tears with wonderful insights. One insight is people can be in the dying process, but then decide they want to continue on in this form, and can come back. What hit me was that my mom died numerous times, and she just wanted to be with us. I felt an overpowering sense of love… the love Mom had/has for her family, and her joy of being with us. I'm sure she is still here in spirit.

At one point Walcsh makes this statement from God:

> *…loved ones can come back to you more than once, out of their sense of wishing to be complete with you.*
>
> *p. 206*

Once again it hit me that my relationship with my mom had been somewhat contentious over the years. Could she have come back several times and stayed with the physical to be complete with me? My heart opens with this thought.

In the end it was my Dad and myself that did much of the physical care along with a paid helper who was indispensable. To be sure, part of Mom's staying was to enjoy the children my sisters were giving birth to, but also I was a big part of her staying. This insight really helped cement my relationship with my family, my participation with them, and the importance of me being with them. They need me. I know they love me, but I also see my importance to their lives, too. I think this realization is what my mom helped create through the last few years of her life.

The gift of my mother's death? What a challenging question to put into words. For 63 of her 65 years of life, Mom had lived in the same Midwest town in Kansas. She loved being involved with everything. When she died people from every walk of life came to say thanks. The love I felt expressed by them radically changed my view of community. This was her last and perhaps her greatest gift.

As I previously mentioned my mother had been very ill, requiring twenty-four hour care that we provided at home for seven years. Her level of care was so high that only three nursing homes in the entire country would even consider taking her. That's right. Not three in the state, but three in the entire country with the closest being nine hours away. So between my Dad and my two sisters we made the commitment to keep her at home as long as we were able.

When mother first came home from the hospital seven years ago, the doctors told us she wouldn't last a year. Mentally her attitude was always pleasant, and she lived in the moment, never complaining. But, physically, she had many challenges the primary one being her breathing. She couldn't breathe on her own and was connected to a ventilator. This meant she could not be left unattended, even for a few minutes. Because that ventilator kept her alive, the slightest change in her breathing would set off loud alarms. Depending on her health that day the monitors might not go off for several hours or they could go off every five minutes. We never knew and were constantly on guard and prepared for when they went off.

Although we had quickly learned how to handle the machine, one of the biggest challenges turned out to be sleeping at night. After a full day of tending to her needs, sleep at night was interrupted continually by the ventilator's alarms. We took turns and shifts although most of the responsibility fell to our Dad.

I was the weekend relief. Driving the three hour drive to their home on Friday afternoons I found myself in a mix of glad to be giving my Dad a break and dreading the constant alertness that the next forty-eight hours would require. These weekends were emotionally draining, although at the time I didn't have time to feel this. But, in retrospect I realized how much it had taken out of all of us. Keeping her alive required everything we had to offer, and after seven years, I was exhausted on all levels - mentally, physically, and emotionally. And yet we kept on. My Dad had bought her a big pink Energizer bunny that she loved. And we all laughed because it was so true, she just keeps going and going and going. She loved it!

Mom actually died in a hospital that was nine hours from our home. She had just been transferred there the week prior via Life Flight which could be quite an adventure in itself even without being so ill. It was such a difficult decision to have her go to a facility, and dreadful to think of her being transferred by herself without her family helping with the process. So my sister decided at the last minute to hop the flight with Mom. The entire time my mom is strapped to a board, being maneuvered in and out of small spaces. It was loud and uncomfortable to say the least. When they got off the plane, my sister was exhausted beyond belief. My mom looks at her and says with a smile in her eyes and on her lips, "What an adventure!" That image and experience stays with me and is the call to my heart when I feel worn down by life. No matter how hard something is, experience it and make it an adventure.

Mom was there a week, and already had been moved from the skilled care facility to the hospital due to her deteriorating condition. So Dad and I, along with one of her long-term caregivers, piled into the car to go see her. Being such a long drive I wanted to help with the driving and to share that time with my Dad. It felt so good to have the caregiver with us and all going together. We all were anxious to get to the hospital and see for ourselves just how she was doing and that she was being well cared for.

A block from the hospital we received a call from my youngest sister. She had just received a call from the hospital, telling us Mom had died.

A block away! We were shocked with disbelief and yet on some level relieved that it was all over. After minimal talking we drove on in silence. We just wanted to get there.

After parking we made our way to the ICU where the doctor offered kind condolences. Mom had actually died several hours before, but the hospital staff had not been able to reach anyone. It was such an incredible gift that we did not have to finish the last few hours of that drive knowing Mom was dead.

We were able to say goodbye to Mom's body in the morgue. We all knew and could feel that Phyllis was no longer present, but her Spirit was living on. I was happy to be there with my Dad, to hug him while he cried and said goodbye to the woman he had loved for forty-five years. I don't remember the exact words said but we found comfort together and said goodbye.

After signing paperwork we made our way to the hotel, promptly went to the small bistro in the hotel and ordered the most expensive wine and meal and began the celebration of Mom's life. She would have loved it! She was always about enjoying life, and celebrating the moment. And this was indeed her moment in time.

The week following her death I experienced love in a way I did not know was possible. I loved having a full day with my siblings and Dad to remember, laugh, cry, be quiet, whatever range of emotions we had to express. No husbands or kids to distract us, just the family she created.

Then almost immediately people began bringing food. They hugged us, and said a few things, and kept moving. Friends of each of us began arriving from all over the country. I was in total amazement of the love and compassion that flowed from everyone. I was in incredible awe. This was not a physical love that poured out rather a deep heart love, unconditional and magnificent. Mom's last gift was one of love – eternal, everlasting love.

Many people from many walks of life had loved Mom. They came and told stories of her generosity and love towards them, how her laughter and acts of kindness had touched their lives.

Most of the time when someone has died I attend the funeral, but not the rosary. Well! The rosary was the night before the funeral, and during the praying of the rosary I really felt uplifted, and felt the vibration of God as experienced through group devotion. I felt like I was chanting prayers. It was beautiful, and my heart was happy and blissful. I had entered true community on many levels but most of all I could feel it here with these people.

During my tumultuous early twenty's I had felt cutoff from Catholicism, so much so that I had stopped attending church and found other ways to commune with God. I realized during this mourning process, being embraced by the Catholic community that I had grown up in, that the rituals of religion are vastly important. These rituals celebrate and commemorate the events of our physical lives. They are rites of passage and recognition. They help to define who and what we are and what we are becoming.

I was so happy to see and be embraced by family and friends. I hugged and cried with friends whose parents had died the year prior. I had attended those funerals, shared in their grief at that time, and now with an open heart mourned and grieved the passing of my mom. In so many ways this was and still is the greatest gift I received—having an open heart and allowing love to enter freely.

After the rosary we had a party at my mom and dad's house. And what a party it was! I had wondered what we were going to do with all the food people had dropped off. Ha! Everyone ate and drank, laughed and cried, and celebrated Mom.

Even though it was early March the weather was warm enough for people to hang out on the deck outside, which was great because not everyone could fit in the house! Two parish priests stopped in and shared a beer with us. Everyone moved from group to group sharing Phyllis stories. It was raucous, and a blast to see my Dad surrounded by friends, some who had moved out of state and came back just for the funeral. They shared great stories about the fun and wild times they'd all shared with my mom. Mom's love of life and love of celebrating life flowed through everyone there that night. Her spirit was definitely there. She would have loved that party, and it gave us permission to celebrate her life, and not dwell on the sadness of her departure.

My definition of community has changed. I look for ways to be of service. My mom did this throughout her life, and I saw how much it meant to so many people. Someone needs a visit in a nursing home? I'll go! Someone's in the hospital because of an attempted suicide? I'll go! Food is needed? I'll bring a dish! I now have a brighter outlook on life, and participation in it. I am now more fully present.

Thank you, Mom!

FIVE

How Deeply You are Connected to My Soul

Kathryn Kilpatrick

There are so many gifts given to us in our journey. Some are obvious right from the start; others reveal themselves bit by bit when the time is right and when we are ready for a deeper reconnection to our soul. There is hardly a day goes by that I do not reflect on the relationship with my mother and the influence she had and continues to have on who I am today and the work I have chosen. It is fascinating looking back to see how the parts and pieces wove together to create this story of our journey together.

Florence Baldwin Mitchell (her married name) was born in 1918 and graduated from high school at the age of 14. Being very bright reflected in her love for reading, her puzzles, writing letters and her high value of precise articulation. Florence was the Mom who would correct you especially when you used a word she felt inappropriate for a situation. This extended even into my adulthood. In her later years she shared that one of her teenage friends was severely hearing impaired so Mom became a stickler for pronunciation and clear enunciation. As mom aged, she struggled with a significant hearing impairment herself. She became very annoyed when people did not slow down their speech or clearly enunciate their words. She had an amazing talent for good grammar and spelling accuracy. I lovingly referred to her as Mrs. Webster's Dictionary. Sounds like the perfect proofreader to me. I surely could use her help proofreading this story. How synchronistic it was that I chose the career I did as a speech and language pathologist. As they say, the apple did not fall far from the tree.

Mom proofread each of the products, articles and columns that I wrote. I have fond memories of her sitting at my kitchen table with me one afternoon as we proofed a reminiscence calendar. It took me back to the many hours I spent at the kitchen table carefully putting together my school projects decades ago! Now it was my kitchen table. She was proofreading and reflecting on events from her younger years. As I listened to her stories, I asked her what she thought about the calendar and the products. I was unprepared for her response. Mom was in total awe of what I was doing. I had a sense that she felt if it had been a different time this could have been her. I am so grateful that she made that comment because it triggered in me a deep feeling of gratitude for all that she was and how that had been the basis for my ability to do what I do.

I made Mom an integral part of my work. How I came to do what I do made sense in a new way for me. How interesting life is; it was feeling like we had come full circle. I felt so very blessed. Little did I know this was just the tip of the iceberg.

In the last 10 or more years of her life, my mom developed a mild hearing loss that progressed to a rather major loss through her remaining years. Later she fell and lost the sight in one of her eyes. She was a trooper. In the many days I spent with her after the surgery to try to restore her vision, I watched her cope with another sensory loss and redefine her life, giving up some independence for a period of time. Relying on others was not her style. Her independent spirit, her innate inner strength and the love and support of her family helped her to continue to live a full life. She was blessed in many ways and provided us a role model for independence and innate strength through some of the challenges she faced. As the oldest child I sometimes wonder about how I will handle this in my later years.

I knew in my heart of hearts that my mom greatest fear was that she might have Alzheimer's disease in her lifetime since her father had "senility" as it was called in the 1960's. He died very shortly after being institutionalized. Mom's greatest pride was her vocabulary and her ability to use it effectively in speaking and in writing the many letters to friends all over the country.

When she designated me as her health care power of attorney I wanted to be sure that I was upholding her wishes. So it was that we sat at my kitchen table and I asked her specific questions based on my years of experience with older adults and end of life issues to discover her choices at a time when she had no major health problems. Mom was from a generation where going to a nursing home was a major fear. It was not an easy task but eventually we created a document that stated her wishes with particular attention to the area of Alzheimer's disease. Together we created possible scenarios to designate her wishes in the event of a variety of health situations. It was essential that this document would honor her heart's desire without my influence. To develop this prior to any concerns at all was so helpful in her later years. It is not easy to do, but much easier when done proactively. I never even gave it a second thought that these actually scenarios would apply many years later. It just seemed like the right thing to do.

At this time I started a new company, which focused on enhancing the quality of life of older adults and supporting their families, friends and caregivers. My mom and her communication challenges became an integral part of my presentations. As John Stuart Mills once said,

There are many truths of which
the full meaning cannot be realized
until personal experience brings it home.

As the years passed and things changed for her, I would often flash back in my mind to a trip we took in celebration of her 80th birthday to visit my son, who had recently moved to California from Ohio. Sitting on the bed in our hotel room, she shared with me her reluctance to participate in conversations with people. As a woman who prided herself in the world of words she shared her frustrations from not being able to hear clearly. She was afraid of making a fool of herself and said she preferred to just sit and catch what she could in the conversations. To this day that image of us sitting on the bed and hearing those words keeps coming back to me. In retrospect I wonder if she had an inner feeling perhaps that more than a hearing loss was happening.

Mom was so detailed, organized, efficient and socially appropriate, I sense she noticed changes she could not put into words. It seemed that her hearing loss was getting worse but it ended up indeed being more than that. Hindsight is 20/20. We were about to embark on a whole new journey together and an opportunity for me to learn so much more about life, people and change. It gave me an opportunity to learn more about who I was and how I would handle some challenging circumstances.

During this time, I started to expand my work in the areas of dementia and Alzheimer's disease, creating more products to meet the needs of caregivers, health care professionals and families. I felt that what was lacking were tools that would help them enhance the quality of time with their loved ones, especially as their capabilities changed. I began to develop new programs for families and caregivers, and trained to be a volunteer at a local

Hospice organization so that I would have the needed skills to help families walk the entire journey with their loved ones.

Concurrently, little changes with my mom began to become apparent but I was not sure if it was normal aging, her hearing loss or some depression. As I tell the families I work with, the early stages of dementia are very inconsistent. I began to realize our conversation in California had a deeper meaning. Was my Mom experiencing what is now referred to as mild cognitive impairment? My deeper knowing was telling me that we might be preparing for a journey together that would significantly impair her most valued assets. I really could not believe this was happening. I also knew every person is so very different and I was sad and yet felt in awe of the synchronicity of it all. I prayed to be given the insights to do whatever I could to maximize the quality of her days and provide her with the emotional support through the fears I saw emerging. I hoped to be able to smooth the way. I knew I would do whatever it took to do this from out of town. I felt both sad and humble.

The hearing loss appeared to masked her increasing difficulty to respond appropriately. She wore a hearing aid but it was only partially helpful because of her poor hearing discrimination. It was harder to get her to understand what was being said during our weekly telephone chats. I missed having more in depth conversations. I had to keep it very superficial and I felt a growing disconnect. My solution was to put a fax machine in her apartment in Massachusetts so I could send her a short letter to read then call her later and chat. This gave her the information so she was then able to follow the conversations more easily. It helped me to feel more connected at times across the miles.

At the time of my 50th birthday I had organized a life story journal for Mom and asked her to complete it as a gift to me. She seemed stuck and had not gotten very far in the two years since it was given to her. When she came to visit in Ohio that summer I saw an opportunity to help capture my mom's story. I realized it probably was not going to happen unless we did it together and that sharing the story with someone might make it easier for her. As we drove back to her home in Massachusetts she shared her stories prompted by the questions in the journal. I taped her answers. Mom shared many stories and many things I did not know were learned in the process. How incredible to spend many hours in a car being a captive listener. The car was filled with her life stories, the ups and downs. I learned about the woman beneath the stories. Missing however were some of the memories of my childhood years and those of my siblings and at the time that did not make a lot of sense to me. I was disappointed to not know more but grateful for what she had shared. Although I felt emotionally exhausted and drained by the end of the trip, I understood a little better why she had not been able to just sit down and write.

As with any of us, there were paths chosen, roads not taken and all of the emotions of a lifetime. In the listening I walked her journey with her and I understood so much more. How privileged I was to be the recipient of those stories. It was not too many years later that I realized how blessed I was to have made that choice of the taping and the car trip home at that time.

Little things began popping up on my radar screen that just did not fit. When we were away on a vacation in Maine we were playing our traditional games of Scrabble. I noticed some odd things happening with placement of letters and realized that she was having trouble coming up with words and even occasionally misspelling a word here and there. This was not my Mom. I had also noticed that in the proofreading she was missing more and more items. It was at that moment that the bigger picture flashed in front of me. My biggest fear that she might become one of the people I talked about and had worked with on some level for over 30 years was beginning to materialize. The pieces of the puzzle started to come together. Little things that had happened that seemed out of character made some sense and years later ever more so. On one level it was very important to take what I was seeing, process it and use the skills I had gained through decades of work to help my mom. As a daughter I prayed to be given the insights on how to best ease her fears and maximize her strengths for as long as possible.

How synchronistic that I began a new endeavor called Communication Connection at that time. Its purpose was to enhance the quality of life of the older adult and support their families, friends, and caregivers. I was now talking about me, my mom, my family. Balancing the roles of knowledgeable professional and caring daughter was one of the most amazing and challenging gifts Mom ever gave me.

Initially in presentations, I gave tips on how to better communicate with those having hearing difficulties. Everything I knew from years and years of experience was being fine-tuned. Even using the most appropriate strategies, they did not always work with Mom. Being over 600 miles away I was constantly revising them and learning what worked best with my Mom while learning how to stay connected across the miles. This was so important for both of us and had the added benefit of something I could pass along to others.

Looking at the larger picture without knowing for sure what was happening, my siblings and I agreed moving Mom into an assisted living environment seemed to be in her best interest sooner rather than later. Throughout this process, I tried to remain centered on the larger picture. That was often difficult as this was MY Mom. My main concern remained to protect and support her independence as long as she was safe. I realized on a personal level what I had seen with so many. Each of us has a unique path in this journey we call life. Each of us has different lessons to learn and attitudes we embrace for personal growth.

There were so many gifts as the last six years unfolded. Mom did not want to move into assisted living. She felt she was totally fine in her apartment. The discussions about this were only upsetting to her. They were upsetting for me also as I wanted to smooth the way for her. I had much to learn from her.

Christmas of 2001 was so memorable to me. I discovered that Mom was teaching me a new way to approach difficult conversations. My daughter approach was not working and I found myself shifting into my professional mindset. Although I had worked with these same situations every day for years and years, now it was my life and our journey together… time to change my words to reflect my heartfelt wishes. Rather than telling Mom what was best I started planting seeds of concern.

We visited a senior residence affiliated with the church of my youth. While there we ran into several residents from the church who had made the choice to leave their homes. Mom had the spontaneous opportunity to talk with them. We planned to return for a lunch after the holiday.

One evening returning to her apartment after a dinner out with my brother and his wife, Mom told me that she had decided it was time to move into an assisted living facility. It was the best Christmas present ever! I said prayers of gratitude over and over. I know how hard that decision was to make but SHE had made it and I was there to hear those words.

Interestingly, as I read through her Christmas cards and the many letters she received, there were more than a few from friends that talked about moving into residences so as to not burden their families and notes from others who had made the move. I felt blessed that everything was in perfect order and I was so very grateful that I had been there for Christmas. As a health care professional, I knew this proactive move would enhance the quality of her life. Although she was losing some independence, she would be safe. As a daughter, I was feeling the sadness she had and some of the fear she was expressing about her forgetfulness. As for myself there was a sense of relief that she would be safe; yet also, a sense that in her acceptance of this move she was acknowledging another loss of one small part of her independence. What a bittersweet feeling of awareness and growing acceptance on my part.

It took many months before the move happened. She began vacillating but then an incident occurred and the move went ahead. I decided that I could be more helpful if I came out a few weeks after the move. There was plenty of family there to handle the actual move and support her through that process. My sense was my help would be needed in other ways and that would become clearer once she had a few weeks of time to herself in her new environment.

Mom settled into a very lovely apartment made comfortable with her furniture including the bed she and my dad had shared. Her assisted living allowed family to stay over night. Because the bed was two twin beds on a single headboard, I was able to stay in her room. Since I would be staying with her for over a week it was also an opportunity to address any concerns that might arise once the reality of the move had settled in. We both needed the time together to reminisce and explore her new options, and learn ways for her to move ahead at her own pace. I needed the time to adjust to mom's contracting physical world and my sense of what could be on the road ahead. This is where the knowledge helps but also makes it much harder on another level. At times

I just felt numb and so very sad for her as I sensed her fear of more losses.

Life had changed so much. My mom was very organized and detailed; yet, I saw a woman who was overwhelmed with where things were. She was not able to organize the way she might have. Change and a lot of activity is not a friend to those with memory loss. I shopped for little baskets to help organize her things, wrote down where items were stored. I learned how to change my pace and my relationship with her. I remembered reading an article that said the 11th commandment was "Thou shalt not parent thy parents." It was a tape that always ran in the back of my mind. I learned to slow down, meet her needs at her pace as I attempted to do for her what I have done for years with my clients and patients. Now I was living what I had taught to so many. With one eye on mother's comfort and the other eye on my growing awareness of decreasing independence slowly creeping in, we shared this time together in ways different from what it used to be and that was okay. I realized this really was about meeting my Mom where she was and not trying to hold on to what used to be. We were living in the moment whatever that moment was, relishing being together and trying to move into solutions with whatever came up. Whenever I visited I was mindful of trying to give her some special moments and me some memories I could cherish years later.

Proofreading was very important at this time as it gave Mom a sense of importance and being needed. Although I could not longer count on her to catch all of the errors, she looked forward to her assignments and this helped to keep her mentally engaged. She still did her puzzles, read her books, and was social at meal times. She had never been much of a joiner. Now that she was hearing impaired and had some memory problems, she was even more reluctant. I explained this to the staff at her residence making some simple suggestions to assist her. I frequently did presentations to the residents, staff and families when I was visiting her. I smiled to hear her promoting a talk to someone or showing her friends my books.

When Mom decided to stop volunteering for the Red Cross, she said it was because of the steep staircase and some other medical problems. I had a sense that the new system of accounting they were putting in was something she could not handle. It was sometime later that she shared that it was primarily because of the difficulty she was having learning new procedures on the computer that she made her decision. In retrospect I marveled at the grace and dignity with which she handled many of those changes. She was coping in her own way and that allowed me to find my place as her daughter.

Although I had many assessment tools I could have used I never tried to test her capabilities. I certainly did not want to make her any more self conscious than she already was. I just wanted to be with her and support her as the changes continued. Sometimes I misread her cues and could see the overload in her eyes. Sometimes I did not catch things in time and she got upset or annoyed. Together we learned and grew quickly forgiving each other's shortcomings. My years of experience contained a wealth of solutions that I was able to tailor to her needs while honoring her journey.

Seeing and knowing her to be safe, I was better able to not get caught up in Mom's drama of everyday living. Instead I found myself following the advice of a wise therapist who said, "Go to the balcony and observe. You will be able to make healthier choices." These are trying times for families and ours was no different. As with any situation, there were differences of opinion amongst family members and the journey of finding what was best for her became a personal one. Each of us had a different relationship with Mom and each of us needed to find our own way. Throughout her journey my Mom expressed deep gratitude for all that was done for her. She was quite blessed and I believe each of us took away from those years our own lessons and memories. Going home as often as possible was a choice I made and an important part of MY journey of growing acceptance of what is and expanding compassion for myself, my Mom, my family and others.

Balancing my personal life in another state, holding onto a job, writing and creating a new company and being present with Mom was a real challenge. Although it took its toll in some ways, I would not change one thing. My admiration of Mom's ability to remain a very classy lady under trying circumstances grew. One day we were out at lunch as her treat. When the charge slip came, instead of filling in the tip and signing it, she simply and gracefully passed the slip over to me to fill in the appropriate amount for the tip and add it up. The moment flowed effortlessly as if this was a normal occurrence. Another change handled by her with great pride. That was my Mom! Her many ways of coping with her losses in functioning through the years has been etched in my soul and flash through my mind more often than I would have ever imagined. Mom was amazing!

Mom's driving ability was the next major difficult conversation topic that needed to be addressed. Attempts to have the discussions about driving were getting nowhere and no one wanted to take her keys away. I was coming home at Christmas again and I knew that something needed to happen as soon as possible. She was more and more at risk to herself and other drivers.

Mom taught me so much the previous Christmas. I tried a similar approach that would afford her the most dignity. I talked about my concerns with her driving rather than telling her what to do. After planting the seeds, I went to visit a cousin out of town for a few days. Upon my return we shared the things she would miss if she did not have a car. I offered easy solutions for things she needed from the store, transportation, concerns for hair and medical appointments. After the seeds were planted I did something hard for me at times, I stopped talking about it!

Christmas Eve Mom said she had something to tell us. Her words said it all – "It is my choice." She had never had an accident or a ticket in 68 years but never had wanted to jinx it by saying anything before. She never once complained once she made it be her decision. Another wonderful Christmas gift! I was so in awe with all that I was learning while I also ached over how very hard this particular change had to be for her. She did it with such class and I was so very proud of her.

For my niece's wedding she made the plane trip with family to Dallas from Massachusetts okay but was wiped out that first evening. After she rested we went to the party that evening and she did fine. Her confusion was more evident the next day. Her dress was on backwards and inside out and she was wearing my eyeglasses. My heart sank. I told her the dress was on wrong; she told me that was how it was on the hanger. I told her I must have put it on wrong, fixed it and told her I would clean her glasses for her. My relaxed approach rubbed off and she was cool, calm and relaxed. When I got dressed, I closed the bathroom door, ran the water in the sink and bathtub, flushed the toilet and cried my eyes out. We got to the wedding, but I was an emotional wreck. It was worth it when she walked down the aisle and seemed so serene. I was so grateful I was there to help.

Mom's functioning had taken another significant decline. In her own environment she functioned well, taken out of her environment that was not the case. I also knew she would never be able to visit my home in Ohio again and sit at that kitchen table with me. I do not think I ever got over that. We had made many little trips through the years and I cherished those times we spent together. And it would never be again.

Each new awareness brought a heightened sense of loss and gratitude for an abundance of little memories sprinkled through the years we were blessed to have her with us.

One day she wanted to go to the cemetery to see Dad. When we got there the Police had blocked off the entrance, as three bears were loose in the cemetery. Back at the assisted living for dinner I suggested she tell them our unusual happening for the day. When she told me to tell it I realized that she was losing additional capabilities… another lesson learned. Knowing the course of the disease made it easier in many ways and harder in many others… another gift for my professional growth. I needed to stay focused on the present moment…another gift for my personal growth.

The next day I suggested she check out the paper and let me know if it was okay to return the cemetery. She found the article, but she read it to me. My heart just sank. Oh no, I thought. She cannot retell what she read. When I left that time I felt somewhat heavy hearted as reality set in. The Mom I knew was still there but so many parts I had taken for granted were disappearing and I could do nothing to stop the process. Centering in the moment I consciously chose to do my best to be with her at a level that worked best for her as often as I could.

It was the last Christmas I spent with Mom that she bought the red hat. I was doing a speech for a Red Hat gathering and she wanted to get me a hat. I thanked her but told her I would get one when I got home. A day or so before I was going to go back home I realized that I would love to do that speech wearing a hat she got for me. I will forever be grateful for that change of heart. What it would mean for me later on I could never have imagined.

Spring and the ensuing months started to wear on her after she broke her hip and experienced a drug overdose. I came home more frequently and my tiredness was more apparent. There were so many instances in those visits where the toll of the Alzheimer's Disease was more and more visible. Mom was more tired and our time together was much quieter. Writing became more of a problem. When we played Scrabble, she struggled to come up with words, keep score or even be able to spell them correctly but it was important to her to play so we did. Those memories remain very vivid in my mind. I was able to finish my book *Walking the Path to Memory Fitness One Week at a Time* and dedicated it to her. I was also able to acknowledge all that she had contributed to my life at a presentation at her assisted living.

She knew what was happening but the light was going out. She still kept up a good front. A part of me just felt very sad and yet very privileged to be having these profoundly moving yet simplistic moments with her. Perhaps this is what life is really about, the profound yet simple moments together.

One morning we took our water bottles, sat in the gazebo, and just chatted. No running around doing but rather being together. I was so glad that even as tired as I was that I took the time to be there with her. How ironic that simplifying and slowing down the pace was what was in her best interest and it became a great gift to me. This was another memory

I found myself treasuring and learning from years later. These are the stories I use in my presentations. They say - you teach what you need to learn.

At home in Ohio I felt the need to create a morning ritual to help me stay centered. I would get up early, have my coffee and put on the CD *Graceful Passages.* What a calming influence. On some level it allowed me to be more present for the process I was going through.

With sadness I brought her the last book I had written, *Because You Care – What to do when you do not know what to do.* She looked at it and thought perhaps she was supposed to proof read it. She smiled and her words were that it looked nice and when she had more time she would look more closely. My mom had always been such a part of the last phases of each of the works I created. Although she was not a person to give much feedback, I knew she enjoyed helping out. Now I was on my own and I reflected back even more on how we started that journey when I was a child. Visions came back very clearly of the times we played Scrabble and her encouraging me as I did school projects sitting at the kitchen table for so many years. She would always tell me that my report card in kindergarten said I talked too much. It's interesting that the written and spoken words have become my life's work. Our lives were reversing as I encouraged her and assisted her when we were together to retain her dignity and some quality of life.

In late October I noted the progressive changes from the previous Christmas to May then in September and now in October. The change was quite dramatic each time. In subtle little ways I could sense she did not want to do this any more. Knowing the progression of the disease and her current state of overall health, which was good, my heart just ached for her and for myself. It was such a helpless feeling to watch as her mind slowed down and she seemed removed and talked more of not wanting to live this way. The dementia had certainly taken the edge off some of her personality but she knew on some level that she might not be able to remain in assisted living for much longer.

In mid December of 2004 she was taken to the hospital for a variety of problems; she told everyone it was her time and she did not want to live any longer. As much as you may want to honor the wishes of someone, how do you let go? Did it make it easier to handle on some level because I knew that if she lived another year or so she would not possibly know us and would not be able to say her goodbyes? She basically stopped eating. Fortunately she had stated her wishes many years ago that she did not want a feeding tube to prolong her life. She went through a slow but steady decline for the next few weeks and was moved to a rehabilitation center.

After a short time there, it was evident she had given up and the decision had been made to move her to a nursing home with Hospice services. In working with Hospice over the years, I have seen the benefit of what they offer to the person making their transition, but also to families who can benefit from the loving support before and after the death of a loved one. Although Mom's ability to express herself was declining, she was able to express some feelings to various family members that she had held onto for many years. I also hoped that she might have an opportunity to share with one of their staff any thoughts she might need to express that she did not necessarily want to share with family. Her physical comfort as well as her peace of mind in these last days was my greatest wish for her.

When I flew home to help with the move to Hospice, I made sure I packed my red hat! When my dad passed away, I was in the process of a divorce and one of the things I bought to make me feel better was a hat to wear at his funeral. Now I had the hat my mom had bought me – in my favorite color - and I wanted to wear it. Not to mention the fact that in her early years she was a hat lady and looked great in them. Whenever I think of those pictures of her in hats and her impish smile, it touches me in a very special way.

Mom had not seen me since her hospitalization. She wanted me to know that she wanted God to take her and that she was tired and worn out. I hugged her and cried but told her it was okay. When it was time to move her to the nursing home, I rode over in the ambulance with her. She was sitting in a wheelchair and we talked a bit on the way. I brought some of my things inside and then turned around as the attendant was wheeling her in. That moment was a gift from God to me. Here I am as she is crossing the threshold of the one place she has never wanted to be and the attendant takes my red hat and puts in on my mom. Then my wonderful mother tipped the corner of the hat and her head and gave me one of those impish grins. My heart melted with the profound connection at that moment and it helped me watch her cross that threshold with a sense of peace knowing that everything was in Divine Order. Mom knew it and I knew it. What a treasured gift that moment was and still is to this day.

Mom got settled in while I spent time telling the staff her story. Not the medical story but who this person was that we were trusting into their care in what ended up being the last week of her life. This is the work I do for others and now it is my journey. We let her rest and when I came over the next day she did a lot of sleeping. I had brought my *Graceful Passages* CD and books that would nurture me while I sat at her bedside. Although she had a hearing loss and was not wearing her hearing aides I wanted to fill the room with music that had calmed me and that would allow her to be surrounded by messages that would fill her being as she rested for the next part of her journey.

The next day she was more alert and talkative. My sister-in-law and I did a mini worship service with her as we each sat on one side of her. At the end we were all crying and she hugged us and said she wanted to go that day and take us with her. Then she laughed and said no it wasn't our turn. We looked at photograph albums and I told stories. She was having more trouble recognizing pictures.

When they came to bathe her at bedside, I was taken by the irony and beauty of what was happening. Without her glasses, dentures or hearing aide she was allowing the male aide with a heavy foreign accent to bathe her. I know she had not a clue what he was saying and there she is joking and laughing. At a time when her pride could have made the situation stressful, she was in the moment. This gentle man told me what a wonderful woman she was. Yes, she was! In that moment I was never more proud of her and the dignity she portrayed. I had the privilege of witnessing her finest moments… a gift I will never forget.

When I went to leave, to return to Ohio to bring my car back, I told her how I loved her and how proud I was of how she had been in these last years which were so challenging for her. Mom hugged me, and then gave me an incredible parting message. "You do good work. You understand."

Mom had taught me so much these last few years, even with its ups and downs, I know she knew that I had an understanding on a deeper level and did the best I knew how. We had learned together and now this was the beginning of another whole new journey for me.

When I was driving there on Saturday I was not sure I would make it in time but I was actually okay with that. We had said our goodbyes and I really wanted that to be my last memory of her. Others who lived in the area and supported her daily through this process now needed to have their time with her and each other.

Driving through Pennsylvania, I passed the exit called the Lord's Valley and two crows flew in front of the car. Crows seem to be messengers for me and it dawned on me that perhaps I should pay attention to the time. I really expected I would get a call but I didn't until an hour later. I realized on some level I was being told that she was leaving her body shortly and she was letting me know. Several weeks later I was driving down the road and two crows flew in front of me, then shortly another crow flew by. I just smiled!

More than a year later perfect timing was again made obvious to me. One day my answering machine quit, but the recorded messages I had saved remained. In particular was one I saved from my mom shortly after she moved into the assisted living. While a friend was there, the fire alarms kept going off and my mom was sharing all this on the recorded message. She got cotton for them to stick in their ears because it was a system malfunction and not a real fire. Mom was in great spirits and giggling. The very next day I was speaking at a hospital on the topic of aging parents and when to step in. At the end of the program, we were interrupted by the fire alarms and a system malfunction. Later that night it dawned on me that perhaps mom was looking over me, knowing she had been my greatest teacher and that in her challenges I was doing my best to help others walk that journey with a loved one in a way that the gifts are what you recall.

One of the most important things I feel we can do for ourselves and our loved one is to learn to meet them where they are, accept the changes and take as many moments as you can to create memories. I am so grateful I changed my mind and let my mom buy me that red hat.

Whenever I wear it, I think of her with great pride as a woman who ended her journey on this earth with the great class and caring she was known for.

Several months after her passing, a very dear friend called and said she had to give me something. It was a picture from the works of artist Brian Andreas and beneath it was written:

When she wore the hat, even many years
later, she could still smell her mother's
perfume and it was hard to remember
she was supposed to be alone.

Picture two stick figures with the smaller one, under the arms of the larger one, wearing a RED HAT! There is nothing more to say but WOW! Thank you for being my mom and a wonderful teacher.

Each story remembered keeps bringing gifts to me as I continue on my path of personal growth and evolving into another level of the work I believe I am here to do at this time.

Several weeks after the funeral I attended a service at church on the spirituality of the journey with a loved one with Alzheimer's disease. Here was yet another instance of perfect timing. These are the words to a song the presenter played which means so much on so many levels.

Mom, I know you thought I could not carry a tune in a bucket but these words I sing to you in praise and gratitude.

"How could anyone ever tell you
You were anything less than beautiful?
How could anyone ever tell you
You were less than whole?
How could anyone fail to notice
That your loving is a miracle?
How deeply you're connected to my soul"

"How could anyone ever tell you"
Words and Music by
Libby Roderich

SIX

A Cold Day in Kansas

Deanna Naddy

The hardest part was closing the casket and the finality it symbolized. I just stood there and touched mother one last time. It was hard and it was final. Mother's physical form was gone. What remained were memories, feelings and a continuing search … but for what?

My mother, Viola, was just shy of 82 years old. She was the oldest of seven children raised in rural north central Kansas. Her early life was sketchy. She really didn't talk much about it. Evidently, being the oldest daughter, she was the "work-horse" of the family. Her infrequent stories told of a life that was hard and meager. However going through her pictures I found a very different story. There are two that just fascinate me; one is of my mother and a cousin at a young age with her grandmother and the second is of the same three again at mother's high school graduation. It is a portrait picture not just a snap shot and they are dressed to a "tea!" At graduation mother had a car, which was a luxury that not everyone had. So

I remain somewhat perplexed about my mother's early life. It seems like she had some perks. Stories pieced together from different family members indicated she didn't like her mother. I don't know why. I do know she had a difficult relationship with her mother. Her mother was often described as a "spoiled brat." What I do remember is my mother could do anything and everything; and, as a result I always felt inferior.

My memories of my youth include many fun times with my mother's family. It seemed like weekly gatherings of the clan. For me I loved knowing my cousins, aunts and uncles. Much later in life mother shared with me how her mother demanded that all the children show up for Sunday dinner. How much she resented that as, at times, it presented a real hardship to take care of farm chores, family, community responsibilities and show up for Sunday dinner. I was surprised, as I did not consider how that activity might have different meanings for everyone.

Two months prior to her death she was the picture of health. As was her practice each fall she would visit me and she had come and spent two weeks at my home in Tennessee. When she went home she went to the doctor as she was experiencing some stomach distress. She had a long history of stomach problems but we, the three children, were unprepared for finding an intestinal blockage that required immediate surgery. In retrospect, I wonder if mother knew and had spent that last carefree week with me. It was her small reprieve and a plethora of nice memories for me.

Surgery

Waiting in the family waiting room during the surgery, we were very surprised and immediately anxious when the surgeon appeared shortly after the beginning of the surgery. Mother had both stomach and colon cancer with an intestinal blockage. They were not sure which was the primary cancer site. The cancer was so extensive that there was no healthy tissue in the gut so removing the blockage was impossible. They simply put a tube to vent the build up of gas in the intestines and sewed her up. We took her home a few days later.

The shock of the surgery, the diagnosis and the extensiveness of the blockage were over whelming. I first felt helpless and defenseless. Yet, somewhere deep inside an inner strength and calmness I had never known before began to express itself. This deep inner strength was the first of many gifts from my mother in her death and dying.

Initially we had to decide what mother wanted to do and what we could do even though there didn't seem to be many options. Mother wanted to go home. I could see the fear in my two brother's eyes; they knew that I could not stay indefinitely. But that is what we did, took her home. Our commitment to help Mother in any way overrode our fear of how to do it. This inner strength when the way seemed insurmountable came to the surface. We called upon this inner knowingness frequently.

At Home

Home after a week in the hospital, mother, my two brothers and I spent the time talking about "what she wanted" for comfort measures, the funeral and the wake. Her strong belief in God and her abiding inner peace and courage were magnificent. We walked a lot and told stories of growing up and remembering. I stayed with her a week after she went home to get things set up and everyone comfortable with their jobs; my nursing background does come in handy. Hospice was started. My two brothers were to take turns every other day being with mother after I left.

Mother had a good appetite and ate everything even though she had a blockage. We talked about this but she just smiled and continued to eat. I thought that was odd but it just showed her will to live. Mother continued to eat to "keep up her strength."

The hardest part was when I left to return to my home. Mother didn't look at me or tell me good-bye. My last memory of her alive was that morning with her sitting at the kitchen table, her head down, obviously not wanting me to leave. It was almost more that I could bear. I had work responsibilities that I had to attend to. Later I figured she knew we would never see each other again; and, it was too difficult to look at me one last time. For years I felt it was unfair. I really needed her permission to leave. I planned to return in a week AND I wanted that to be okay with her.

Then I began to realize how difficult my leaving was for her, that perhaps she needed my strength to help her face the coming days plus it was possible I would not return in time. My two brothers were equally as anxious with my leaving, as they had to step up and take turns as caretakers. I had prepared them as best I could and we had great support from Hospice. It turned out to be a really great and growing experience for each of them to provide that care and I am sure it was good for my Mom.

Arriving home on Sunday, I turned around and returned to Mother's on the following Saturday. I spoke with her on the phone on Friday afternoon, she sounded in good spirits. I told her that I would be there on Saturday, as I would catch an early flight and someone would pick me up for the four hour drive from the airport. I was totally unprepared to find her in a coma by the time I arrived the next day. She died two days later. My feelings were deep with being cheated, why couldn't she have waited just a few more hours? My two brothers got to say good-bye, yet I had been denied. I felt angry, guilty, so unworthy and yet I was also very aware of my one brother's pain. He had the watch on Friday night when Mom had been in a lot of pain. He was the one to deal with her suffering. I spent those last two days with mother in a coma, observing her breath, trying to reach her, telling her how much I loved her. I felt so physically helpless and almost in a dream as an observer of what was happening and me being unable to change anything, just watching, accepting, and gently releasing mother.

In contrast when Dad died five years earlier, I could "feel" my Dad and talk with him in consciousness, but not so with mother. This puzzled me. When mother was alive I always felt very much supported. I wondered if I was being punished for leaving her. I just couldn't understand. Later in searching for an answer, I went to someone who could contact people who have died. She said that mother was "out playing" and was not to be disturbed. As the oldest sibling she had taken on the caretaker role and had major work responsibilities in a large family growing up and then continuing in her own family.

Now it was her turn to play. This seemed to help me in understanding, but I was still disappointed. This disappointment continued until I gradually understood that she was revealing that she loved me so much that she couldn't bear to see me leave. I found much comfort that she was now getting to play. How fun that must be for her! Perhaps the message is that if you don't get it correct in this life time you will get opportunities in the next so why not try to get it right this time around. I am definitely making more time for FUN! Mother's gifts of insights into me and my life were revealing themselves and continue to grow stronger. As I write this I am hearing an inner voice tell me "but I did come."

Several months following my mother's death I had the film in my camera developed and to my surprise the first picture was of my Mother sitting on my porch swing. What a gift, right on! She did show up. I had even forgotten that I had taken the picture. It was a most beautiful gift then and even more so now.

Mother died about 14 years ago. It feels like yesterday. I know this is "my stuff"- the ruminations of an unsettled physical mind. And that in itself is a tremendous gift – realizing that no matter what mother did or did not do; she did the best she knew how to do. I did the best I knew how to do. There is no one to blame AND my stuff is simply "stuff" that is growing less and less as I continue to grow in inner wisdom and understanding.

The Funeral

Well, you do need to know, I grew up in rural Kansas. The cemetery sits on a flat area looking over rolling hills and nearby farms. There are cedar trees and mostly open space. It is so quiet, so desolate on cold winter days, yet so beautiful in spring and fall.

The casket was closed before we started the funeral service. So many, many people came, so many. When mother was alive so many people came to support her. At the wake and afterwards it was really different. They stopped in at the house, they brought food, but they didn't stay. It was so noticeably different because she wasn't there. It felt almost bizarre. I had a strange empty feeling like part of me was missing. It took a long while and I'm still working on the space that mother's physical death has created in my life. Yet, that space is important far more important that I can articulate at this point. As I focus on it I'm discovering that it's the space that makes the objects, like me, stand out and be recognized. It's the space that gives definition.

My cousins stood up at their parents' funerals and talked about their memories. We could not do that, my brothers and I. It just wasn't our style and outward expression. Interestingly, at mother's 80th birthday party over 350 people showed up. At her funeral a very large number also turned out. My sister-in-law and I wondered at the time if even ten people would show up for our funeral. We continually compared ourselves to my mother. She was the role model of what we have never been – or so it felt. Such a gift to discover that I am just as good as she was and in so many and different ways. It took her death to bring this gift into focus – from unworthy to worthy.

Role Model

Mother had some sort of attraction factor and people just loved her. She had a big open heart and was always helping others. What a role model! It was incredible. She stayed active and didn't give in to her years of stomach problems. She genuinely cared for herself and others. Her faith in God was strong. She was not afraid to live or not live. I observed the inner peace my mother experienced in those last days. Yes, she was shocked to learn she had cancer. But within a relatively short time she came to terms with what that meant. She possessed an inner strength that allowed her to be present and involved with us in those last days. We told stories, took short walks, played games. My mother was the family historian so we tried to get her to reminisce about the "good old days."

Now 14 years later I gain much comfort in having that time to reflect, to be together, knowing that it would not be forever. It changes how one uses time, I remember thinking "I should be doing something really important with this time because my mother is dying and she will not be with us very much longer." It was when I was able to just be present with my mother just talking, going for a short walk, or playing a game of cards or just sitting quietly that nothing else mattered—that was what was important.

It feels more and more that some of those qualities are emerging in me – energy, strength, faith. My faith is different through more expansive. Mother's strong faith was locked into the church and that particular belief. While I go to church I do not find the same solace in my church as my Mother did. My mother's courage helped me to discover that inner peace for myself. I'm finding an Inner Strength that goes beyond the church walls. It's in the deep connection to God/Universe/Eternal Wisdom/ AND it is within me.

In my spiritual search I have learned that we are dynamic energy beings, we effect and are affected by everything around us, and everything in the universe is connected and has an energetic frequency. Consequently intention is extremely important because your intention can change and affect things. Five things for me are critical for living – love, gratitude, forgiveness, intention and presence. These make a great difference in my every day life.

If you are present in the moment the rest is pretty easy. I am grateful to wake up every day to whatever the day presents, grateful for my three sons and their families, for friends, extended family, just about everything. I have discovered that forgiveness resolves more around forgiving my self for my shortcomings and renewing the effort to do better. It is when I turn away from my true self that the judgments and emotions rise up and I recognize that forgiveness occurs on many levels. When I think I have completely forgiven some aspect of my life, something invariable happens that gets an emotional response from me and there it is again. I think love needs no explanation except that I am learning more and more to hold an open heart with love; it is an acceptance of what is and valuing that without judgment. It is a work in progress.

My mother was my lifeline. She was the one I knew that I could count on no mater what. She was gone. My question was; who could I count on? Who was there for me? And yet, this was the springboard for me to go inside and begin the discovery of who I really am… another gift in disguise!

I found myself searching for other things, which were spiritual rather than church. I'm not saying church is not important. It just doesn't completely support and nourish me. I keep discovering on deeper and deeper levels that all of us have Divinity within us. I not only say that but also want to experience that more and more. For me it's about being connected, being present in the experience.

Blessings and Realizations

My Lord! There are so many blessings from mother's dying and death, so many realizations. The first thing was that this event brought my brothers and me much closer. When mom was alive, the family activities centered on each of our connections to her. Now it is with each other. It just evolved and is so wonderful to have that connection.

Mom instilled in us a strong sense of family, I have been blessed with grandchildren who <u>want</u> to come and see me. Family is important. I value that. It was how I grew up and mother has passed that value on to me. I have eleven grandchildren soon to be 12. My 16 year old grandson chose to "hang out" with me for most of last summer.

Oh, yes, my 12 year-old grandson says with pride, "I'm the grandmother who travels." He likes to bring his friends out and show them through the house and all the neat "stuff" that grandmother has collected in her travels. Mother had that kind of relationship with family and extended family – second cousins and even beyond would come to see and be with my mother. My perimeter is not as great as hers, but it's growing!

When I left home to go to college I never lived at home again so I didn't have the experience of living in a community where everyone knew me growing up. The person I married, well, we didn't have a big circle of friends. But now, I have more friends than ever before in my life! That's been one of my goals – to expand that part of my life. I find I always have room for one more friend.

It is difficult to separate my divorce and mother's death as the divorce came soon after her death. It was a time of learning to be able to go out on a limb and look around. I started to do more things for my healing and me. I think it's that gift of curiosity and desiring to be in the world as an active participant that I observed in my Mom. For instance, I spent a week in Montana at a healing retreat with Dr. Andrew Weil. I found counseling to be very helpful getting over those rough times. I joined a women's group to expand my awareness of my self and my relationships. I spent three weeks in Peru studying with a Shaman. I finished my doctorate. I recently journeyed to Mexico to take a two week painting class. I am not afraid of an adventure. Thanks Mom! Still I am continuing to grow and learn and adding new talents. I find that I'm becoming more open to experience – more open to what life has to offer AND, it makes me smile with peace and contentment.

Mother's death clarified a lot of things in my marriage. Upon news of her death my children came immediately to support me. My husband did not as he said he wanted to "remember mother as she was." I wanted, no, needed him to support me at that time. I was crushed. More "stuff" was being made clear to me and we parted company not long after that.

Mothers and Husbands

Interestingly, my mother was supportive of me throughout my life. She must have seen something different in my husband than I did. After her death I found the strength to deal with the Kansas sense of "commitment for life" to a relationship even if it was so destructive. Her long held support of me was bearing fruit. The gifts of strength, courage and wisdom were coming through loud and clear.

Now my former husband and I have a decent relationship. We have family events that mostly occur at my home. Recently when he had heart valve surgery I found myself closely examining my role. Do I go on the planned two-week trip to Mexico or stay home and hover? My role was to go to Mexico and deepen my inner connection. Always before I had been the buffer for my children. They were okay. We all knew that and felt it. Although I didn't want him to die, I realized that I still cared about him in some freakish way – on a deeper, more encompassing, compassionate way. I'm still working on accepting this gift of compassion.

Change and Growth

As I move from a cold day in Kansas further out on the limb a lot of things are happening for me. One of the first awareness's after my mother's death was of being an orphan and suddenly being the next generation… "the one that held the wisdom." I felt so inadequate. I was amazed at those two feelings and how poignant they were. I now was the "older generation" while before I always felt I could draw on my mother's strength and wisdom. Now it was me. Previously while I did rely on myself, I had the cushion of believing I could check things out with Mom if I needed to. I had to digest that one for a while.

I'm doing more things in which I have to be Present in my Truth. My faith is deepening. I'm discovering the gift of space since mother's physical form is gone. That space, that stillness beckons me deeper into Inner Awareness, into Presence. I'm discovering that Presence not only encompasses all people and things, but also is all people and things.

SEVEN

The Amazing Technicolor Dream

Mary Ellen Jackle

On December 16, 1987 at age 72, my mother, Ellen, left this world for the spirit plane. Before that she had Alzheimer's Disease. Everything we encounter in life is a gift if we make it so. At the time, I didn't see the good in anything as tragic and terrible as Alzheimer's. In retrospect, I've learned a lot about myself and our world. The main thing I learned was to appreciate every moment I live, the gifts I have and to enjoy them while I can—not because I have a fatalistic belief that they will be taken away from me some day, but, well, they could be. After all, it happened to her.

Mom was so smart, even with no college education. She was an avid reader with an ever-widening range of interests, including all things metaphysical. In her younger days, she was a librarian, a job that she really enjoyed. And the irony wasn't lost on her that she was a mentor and teacher to the new college graduates, just hired at the library, who learned so much from her and made more money than she ever would. Anyway, she was very proud of her accomplishments and the loss of her mental faculties made her sad and frustrated. Mom, even in later stages of the disease, occasionally had lucid periods during which time she was aware of how much she was loosing. Now I find this is part of the tragedy of Alzheimer's.

So I appreciate what I have, yet at the same time have a deep sense of the transience of things. I'm not a worrier since I "know" much about how the Universe works; still, I sometimes worry that some day, like my Mother, I'll suffer from Alzheimer's Disease. I see myself in her place every time a name or a fact escapes me and that frightens me whenever I think about it. So I pretty much don't think about it.

What I worry about most, I will absolutely attract into my life because the Universe perceives me thinking and dwelling on it. Not being judgmental like humans are and aiming to please, the Universe gleefully sends me whatever has been holding so much of my attention—even if this turns out to be the very thing I most dread. So, the best thing to do is not worry; just "let go, let God," and have faith. Well, even with such remarkable insight, it's easier to say than to do.

Anyway, Mom did worry a lot about "becoming senile." We had no word for Alzheimer's disease in those days. Her inner world, the world of her incredible, brilliant mind, was important to her. She also used to worry that she would die before my father did. He had muscular dystrophy. If she went first, who would take care of him? Of course, both of those things came to pass.

A dear friend once asked me how this gift of Alzheimer's affected me. Again, in retrospect (All right! I'm a slow learner!), I found that Mom's suffering and struggle with Alzheimer's was yet another example of what I've read or heard from a wide variety of sources: that we create our own reality. For example, there is something you must do. You don't want to do it. Like go to work on a gorgeous day. Perhaps you cannot control the situation, but you can control how you *respond* to it. Thereby you create your own reality for that situation, either by being miserable all day at work and making everyone around you miserable or by being sincerely happy, doing your best job, and making others around you happy. Mom chose to do the latter.

Mom never complained about her waning memory. She never wanted to burden her family with it. In fact, she chose to try and hide her ever-worsening dementia as long as she possibly could. During her perfectly lucid moments, it must have been difficult for Mom to go through it alone, especially since we've always been a close-knit family. But she chose to go through it without support or someone to listen to her complaints about it. She chose this more difficult path out of love. We all slowly began to notice the changes she tried to hide. Out of love for her and wanting to support her decision, we played along, pretending not to notice the changes, doing what we could to not disturb her routines, quietly helping her to "pull it off."

On a deeper spiritual level, "creating one's own reality" also means that before my next incarnation into the physical life, my angel and I sit down and together decide what I need to learn in this next lifetime. What is the greatest soul-growth that I need now? Then together we work out how I will accomplish this: in what situations and circumstances will I find myself mixed up, who will I meet along the way, what opportunities will come along that I will either take advantage of (hopefully) or rail against. Then my angel and I hug, and off I go.

Oh, and like most of us, shortly after my arrival here on earth, I'll forget whatever I had decided would be my "life plan," which will make it even more challenging to get to where I had decided that I wanted to go. But with the challenge comes more growth than even my angel and I could have ever imagined! NOT original ideas on my part, but in Mom's time, there was so much less material available to the general public. One couldn't just walk into any bookstore like we can today and find a stack of books about angels and spirit guides. So, Mom worried, and her greatest fears came to pass, whether or not by her own design, or maybe instead by Someone Higher's even more brilliant design. These concepts give me more comfort now as I remember how she bore the sorrow and loss and how she tried in every way that she could to maintain normalcy in her life, in her relationships, and in her struggle to be self-sufficient.

At the time, I handled her losses and her aloneness as best as I could, but I shared very little in her actual Alzheimer's process for two reasons. First, she covered up for as long as possible. I've since learned that "covering up" is so typical of Alzheimer's patients in the early stages of the disease that it is actually listed as a symptom. I feel that because she was so intelligent, Mom was especially talented at hiding her memory lapses. Second, my husband, Bob, and I lived in Ohio while Mom and Dad were in Eastern Pennsylvania. We both had busy jobs and busy lives and were lucky if we "went East" as often as once a month. Plus we split our time visiting my family and Bob's family.

Seeing Mom less frequently we noticed the subtle deterioration in her condition. As long as she and Dad were managing OK in their own home, we would pretend not to notice. Dad was in a wheelchair with his muscular dystrophy and needed help with all activities of daily living. He was also extremely patient and knew how to break down even the simplest of actions into small concrete tasks. He was also good at maintaining their set routines, since anything, no matter how insignificant, that interrupted this routine caused Mom great consternation. When we did come East, we limited our visits to just a few hours and would bring dinner. That way they could relax and enjoy our visit, we'd say. It was its own little routine.

As Mom became worse, she became less and less verbally communicative. She would enjoy just sitting there, listening and grinning, while Dad led the conversations. I missed the little sharings that go on between a mother and daughter; I especially missed the "parlor talks" about all things metaphysical. Mom just loved to get into it! Yet, I could always see the love in her eyes. She always knew us. And she always enjoyed our visits as long as we kept it simple.

She and I got back to the deeper sharing again after she passed over.

Mom and Dad lived for about 20 years in a small ranch house on the side of a mountain with a fabulous view over the town, the rolling hills and the Blue Mountains beyond. They had a patio jutting out from the rear of the house, accessible by sliding glass doors off of the dining room. Many times we would sit outside on the patio, or at the dining room table to talk and enjoy the view.

Mom was physically healthy, had no mobility problems and was as strong as if she worked out at a spa every day. She had no chronic illnesses other than Alzheimer's, and had strong healthy heart and lungs. This was amazing, since she was a smoker. While she and Dad were living at home, she was not yet into her "physical dying process." She was in the dying of her mind process.

But sitting out on the patio or looking out over "the view" from the dining room was a significant part of her living process. Every day she enjoyed "their view." Sunsets were especially favorite times and they never tired of them - nor did I. Perhaps that's why she used that imagery in my first contact with her after she died. Anyway, "their view" was always a significant part of my childhood and it left me with a deep appreciation for the natural world, especially mountains.

Since then, I've traveled far, camped out in some remote places, but our little patio on the side of the mountain, still within the city limits and in a growing neighborhood, taught me that if I cannot escape to some isolated or exotic hideaway, I can still find peace and calm from within myself. This taught me to appreciate even a little patch of green in the middle of a bustling city.

Needlework was another of Mom's passions and she did a lot of it. She did all kinds of needlecrafts including counted cross-stitch and quilting, but her favorite was embroidery, because there are so many different kinds of stitches. She enjoyed learning new ones and perfecting her techniques. Step back a little from her intricate embroidery and it looked like a painting or even photographic. But, as the Alzheimer's progressed, she was no longer able to do even the most elementary of projects. This was a loss to both her and the rest of the family. My already healthy respect for her and her amazing creative abilities was heightened even more as her mind was taking away more and more of her ability to create.

One of my most prized possessions is a small but intricately detailed embroidered picture of a bouquet of lilacs, which Mom had started. As she realized that she would not be able to finish it, unbeknownst to anyone, she gave it to my mother-in-law to finish. After Mom died, I received this beautiful gift started by Mom, finished by my Mom-in-law, and framed by my Father-in-law. Mom gave me an appreciation of my own talents and inspiration to make the best of them – AND a deep appreciation for how beautifully she coped with her losses. It took a lot for Mom to go to my Mother-in-law, not only because they were not particularly close, but also because it meant admitting that she was no longer able to do something that she did well and loved doing.

In the summer of 1987, a fall from her bed resulting in a broken hip meant the end of their life in their own home. Prior to this my brother would check in on them every other day on his way to and from work since he lived only a mile down the road. Mom and Dad went together into a church-affiliated nursing home. Bob and I, living so far away did little to assist in the moving process. Dad handled it on his own, as was his fashion along with all of the transactions involved in selling their house. We came East to visit more frequently. We thought that Mom would hate being in the nursing home and were surprised at how well she took it in stride. This was sometime in late autumn because we had a few picnics together with them amidst the incredible fall foliage on the rather extensive, park-like grounds. Mom was on a locked dementia unit and had close supervision; Dad was in another area in a private room. He was able to visit Mom whenever he wanted.

Recovering nicely from the fractured hip and with her good physical condition, Mom's prospect of a long institutionalization seemed to be in the cards, as it is with the many Alzheimer's patients who are healthy except for the dementia. This is why we all were surprised when she passed over quickly and serenely. The nurse had placed Mom's lunch tray in front of her and briefly assessed that all was well. Mom died during the brief time that it took the nurse to distribute the rest of the lunch trays on the small Alzheimer's wing and return to feed Mom.

I feel that we have more control over the time we leave our physical bodies than is generally believed. The writings of such authors as Bernie Siegel and Elisabeth Kubler-Ross are full of examples. As a nurse I have seen dying patients, even infants, wait until a family member has had the chance to say good-bye one last time. I believe that on some level, Mom knew about her family's sadness and concern for her and was able to decide to take off as soon as possible. This was her parting gift to us. In the moment, even through the grief, I recognized this gift, and have come to appreciate this more and more from the vantage point of time.

When I got the phone call from my brother saying Mom had died, I felt sad, but I also felt a sweet, peaceful serenity and a sense of relief. After all, we had lost the Mom we knew and loved since childhood a long time ago. A strong sense of her presence felt like a reassurance that everything was all right. I knew that the funeral would be difficult, and there would be some difficult times ahead. But the knowledge of her leaving the way she did gave me greater inner strength and enabled me to get through. It was a comfort to me to know that Mom had awareness and even power to be able to leave at her own choosing. There is so much more inside of us that even dementia cannot take away. In fact, what if due to the dementia, as horrible as that was, Mom received a blessed release from *all that thinking*! She may have accomplished a lot during that time when her lucidity was stripped away, maybe akin to being in a constant meditative state of consciousness. At some profound level, she knew *exactly* what was going on, which may be the reason she died so peacefully, at a relatively young age and without a long struggle.

Only a few nights passed after her death before the dreams started. I was keeping a dream journal and had trained myself to remember my dreams in detail, at least long enough to write them down, which I did immediately upon awakening (usually).

The dreams about Mom had to do with a variety of mundane, everyday activities but she was there taking part in them with me. In some dreams, she was confused; in some she was lucid, as if magically cured of her Alzheimer's. In some dreams I would marvel at how that could happen, in others, I would simply accept it. Some of the dreams left me with the feeling that the whole saga with Alzheimer's had been just an illusion.

Father died seven months after Mom died, and then I would dream of the same kind of simple things but with both of them present. Again, these were just general everyday things that did not stick in my memory other than the fact that my parents were with me and that we were enjoying each other's company. At any rate, the dreams were consistent in their ordinariness; none were prophetic or even particularly exciting. Not like the first dream, which I had a few nights after Mom died.

It was a very vivid dream, realistic, with even more intricate details than is usual for me. It never faded and surely would not have, even if I had not written it down for safekeeping!

Mom and I were in a large, bright atrium that looked like an art museum, with a 30–40 foot high arched ceiling. It was lit as if from skylights and the walls also had a soft glow. Mom was proudly and happily showing me one of her newest works. It was all hand-stitched and embroidered and it looked like a tapestry, probably because it was so huge. It covered an entire wall! But all of the stitches were so intricate that they looked like Petit Point - the extremely fine stitches that allow the artist to add delicate details to a picture. (Petit Point can be seen decorating pieces of jewelry such as lockets and brooches. That's how minute the stitches are.) Mom's work was a life-sized picture of my Dad, in silhouette and in profile, looking out over the view from their patio at home, with all the details of the town, the rolling hills and the mountains hazing in the background.

However, the sunset was the most amazing thing. It was something like I've never seen before, with the wildest, brightest, most abundant colors. Colors that one would never think to use to paint a sunset, yet were absolutely perfect. The colors of the sunset were reflected subtly on the mountains, on every building in the view, in the grass in our backyard and even glimmered on the wrought iron patio railing. Best of all, the glow reflected on Dad's face and made his eyes sparkle. Of course, I raved over it with enthusiastic abandon. Mom just smiled and said to me in a voice full of kindness and love, "It isn't for you - yet." As I was trying to explain that I wasn't asking her to give it to me, just expressing my awe and admiration of it, I awoke and felt so joyous that I had to go downstairs and dance. Then, suddenly peaceful and sleepy, I went back to bed, not even worried that I'd forget the dream or lose some of the details. In the morning, I recorded it in my dream journal.

The incredible needlework/embroidery/tapestry, something way beyond what Mom used to create in her earth-life, was her way of illustrating for me what we both believed about the after-life, that between earth-lives we live in higher planes and continue to learn and develop and evolve. We used to have long lively, fun discussions about this. What an example!!

I believe that she really created it, even though she had only passed away a few days prior... since time, as we know it, is only a factor on earth. Or, maybe it was her work in progress but on the astral plane where I believe we met. She was able to materialize the finished product. Maybe that's what she meant by, "It isn't for you - yet." At the time I understood those words to mean that she would be waiting for me with this marvelous prize when I passed from physical life to the spirit world! One thing for sure, similar to people who have had near-death experiences, I now have absolutely no fear of death. The image of Mom's tapestry has helped me through my Father's death soon afterwards and will doubtlessly be there to help me through upcoming losses of loved ones. I've always had a faith in life after physical death, but it never hurts to have it validated!

The dreams that I previously described continued over approximately the first year after Mom died and have become less and less frequent. After Dad died, they temporarily became more frequent. They were very simple, non-vivid, non-dramatic dreams that had the feel of a quiet visit, much like we used to have back home. I get one of these rarely now, and when I do, it just feels like they're quickly "checking in" to reassure me that all is well. I've never tried to contact Mom or Dad in any other meditative way or with a spiritualist. I just figured that they are happily busy with their new lives, that they know that I don't need their company as much or as often as I used to and that when I join them, there will be lots of beautiful tapestries to admire.

EIGHT

As Precious Today as the Day You were Born

Rowena C. Buxton Tauber

It took many years for my mother and me to come to a place where Mum said these words to me from her bed in the nursing home in Nairobi just a few days before she died – eleven days before her 97th birthday. Our journey together was not always easy. Mum was an alcoholic. However, this story is not about the effect this had on my childhood when my own impression of Mum was severely distorted by lack of understanding. Indeed it was not until I acknowledged my own alcoholism some twenty plus years later, and, with gratitude, joined a twelve step program myself that it even dawned on me that I had played my own part in our horrible relationship. During the course of working my twelve steps I accepted the fact that I was completely responsible for my own actions - no matter how justified I felt about having behaved as I often did. I had a choice.

And thus it was on one of my annual visits to Kenya a couple of years after entering the 12 step program in the United States that I made my own amends to Mum and accepted my part of our relationship. I cannot begin to describe what it felt like to have Mum say a simple but sincere "I'm sorry." My goodness what a way to learn the importance of those few words and allow them to stand alone.

This was a turning point and from then on our relationship began to blossom. Slowly and cautiously we moved into the close and loving companionship that we shared for the last years of her life as she was dying.

As Mum and I became more honest with each other and could share our joys, hurts, concerns and fears, Mum started to tell me stories of her childhood and on through her life with her first husband and then with Dad. Mum and Dad were passionate, interesting, vibrant, courageous and adventurous people. Their relationship had great depth. However, this was a union that brought disgrace and dishonor to Dad, who was an officer in the British Colonial Civil Service. Dad was excelling and destined for a rapid rise to senior positions. Both Mum and Dad were still married and not yet divorced. Dad's career came to an abrupt end. All this was kept from my sister and myself who were the offspring of this marriage. It was only in the last ten years of Mum's life that she started to allude to the stigma that had been attached to them for that relationship.

Since Mum's death and my return to Kenya some of the details have been revealed by friends and from historical records published in the many books written about Kenya's early days and the people who came from England to develop the Colony. It is a tribute to their bond that they weathered this storm and went on to have wonderful adventures and times together.

Whatever their challenges Dad taught me the importance of loyalty to one's spouse no matter what; and, Mum taught me the importance of being true to oneself and holding ones head high regardless of what others are saying about you – for no one really knows what is behind anything. This she was to repeatedly demonstrate to me in her quiet elegant way as she moved deeper and deeper into the dying process. So now I find these gifts of compassion towards others plus living my truth coming forward in my life.

Mum was a gardener and her eyes spotted plants of a special nature wherever she went. Some plants even found their way into her pockets or bag and then into her own garden. Her gardens were creative and filled with unusual specimens. Within her traditional, but not formal, gardens she would include a wildflower garden. Her green thumb ensured that plants relocated to her special areas survived. The Kenya Horticultural Society's various branches would come from many miles to visit her gardens – either the one in the highlands or the one at the edge of the Indian Ocean. Even when Mum could no longer walk she would be carried round the garden in a chair on two poles. While I did not take an interest in gardening while Mum was alive that does not seem to matter for I know she is guiding me now. There is something immensely honoring about friends who knew Mum now saying to me "Oh you're becoming a gardener like your mother." In truth this will take many years and I am working on it.

It was when Mum and I were doing chores together – clearing out the attic for instance - that she would share stories of her life. I began to understand and appreciate what an amazing woman she was. She led her life fearlessly, accepting challenges and tackling whatever came her way. She loved to explore. The friends she met along the way – new friends, old friends, made her travels more interesting. She kept in touch with these people all over the world. At Christmas she would receive Christmas cards from far flung places and from people that I had only heard of through the stories she told of her experiences here and there – Laos, Australia, Taiwan, China, Yemen, South Africa… the varied list continues.

Mum was methodical. While it was difficult as a child to appreciate her desire for tidiness at 2 o'clock in the morning when Mum had drunk so much she could barely walk or speak, I now value what it was she had hoped to instill in me. Everything had its place.

There was a strange dichotomy in Mum's approach to people. She enjoyed "interesting people" who could be of any race, creed or color. It mattered not what someone did with their lives; Mum was interested and asked questions. However, she was intolerant and judgmental of those that somehow did not fit the "interesting" category. She was at least honest about what she felt even though this was embarrassing, especially if these happened to be my friends! Mum loved to entertain and her weekend lunch parties were legendary. She had a knack for introducing guests with similar interests and many a friendship was spawned on Mum's verandah.

To put together a disparate group of friends for a lunch gathering, for instance, takes a sort of courage I find I do not have. Mum had lots of general friends, more than acquaintances but not intimate friends. I do not know if this is a perception or if it was real. I sometimes look at my friends and feel close to them all; and yet, recognize that I have not learned how to have special friends. I often wonder if this is another aspect of a parent being a role model or if this is an inevitable by-product of being both a recovering alcoholic and child of an alcoholic. Mum's gatherings though were a wonderful place to learn to talk to almost anyone thereby finding a common ground to pass a limited amount of time.

Mum had a pioneer courage that was given an opportunity to thrive in Kenya. As a teenager she and her youngest sister were taken there by their parents. For reasons I do not know, her father left them in Kenya to fend for themselves. Grandmother opened a secretarial school in Nairobi while Mum was sent to be a companion to an old man who lived alone on a large farm a couple of hundred miles from Nairobi. She had to get there by ox cart. At the farm she had to run the house, drive the farmer around and assist with the farming – all at the age of 16. These early experiences, and many others, developed in her this incredible ability to live in completely isolated environments. She developed our property on the Coast almost single handedly as Dad had to be away in the forests during the turbulent era before Independence. She built roads, shot snakes, brought up orphaned animals – cheetah, auger buzzards, mongooses to name but a few. She had a sense of bravery and lack of personal fear that defies description.

I hope when my journey is ending I will have the same ability to face my death with the same sense of bravery and dignified acceptance. I was able to experience what a gift that was to those who visited Mum in her declining years. She did not dwell on what she was going through rather she wanted the visitors to tell her what was going on with them. She was always interested, listened intently and asked poignant and penetrating questions. These are useful lessons in my daily life now not just at the end.

Mum did love to travel and wanted to see as much of the world as she could – but not in a tourist group. As our relationship healed we enjoyed many traveling experiences together – trips all over Kenya in search of some special wild flower in its natural habitat, adventures in Bahrain, Iran, Cyprus and exploring some of England together. Her lovely sense of the ridiculous saved us much anguish as we found ourselves in this or that predicament in foreign countries – a trait I attempt to emulate myself in my own travels and in my life.

This desire to explore our planet has since rubbed off on me. In my travels I have felt quite safe being open to whatever experience comes my way. Perhaps my greatest leap of faith was to accept a one-way ticket to the United States from a couple I had met while traveling in China. I did not know what I would do although I knew that with the gift of this ticket would come support in some form. Indeed the gift did come with all that and I feel privileged to have spent over twenty years in the States, thirteen of those under the protective eye of my benefactors.

I met and married a very special man, Fred, in Los Angeles within a couple of years of my arrival there. Several months after my husband died at our home in Tennessee I visited Mum for one of our yearly visits. This time I came with the gift of having received grief counseling from a marvelous counselor at Alive Hospice. Knowing that Mum was tired and wanting to continue her own journey to other realms I had discussed my feelings about this with the Alive Hospice counselor. That December Mum and I had a very special two weeks together. I stayed in a spare room in the nursing home, as I always did on my annual visits to Mum. It was during this visit Mum told me that she wanted to die now and would like me to be with her. She did not feel she could do this in the two weeks scheduled for this visit and thus I made the commitment to return to the States and prepare to join her for an extended visit.

Even after Fred died I had not considered a return to Kenya. I had made my home in the States among my friends there. However, when Mum herself asked me to come back to Kenya to be with her when she died, I felt this was the right thing to do. It was a big decision to honor Mum's request and it is with gratitude that I was given this opportunity. Mum just felt it would be best if I came back to Kenya and take over here where she was leaving off. Although she guided me that way and it did feel right, I missed my life in the States; however, I now recognize the circle that is completed by my return to Kenya.

Previous to this Mum had not mentioned that she wanted to die nor that she wanted me to be with her. When she was 80 she broke her hip, in an alcohol related accident, and was put into the hospital in Mombasa for a hip replacement. This was the first of various emergency visits I was asked to make to assist her recover enough to come out of hospital. Of my siblings I was the one usually called as I did not have children and the perception was that meant I could drop everything. Ultimately this was a major factor in my losing my job. That is yet another story. On the last occasion when Mum was in her late 80s and in hospital with pneumonia I was called again and told that Mum had but a few days to live. This time my sister and brother also came out to be with her. By now I had a strong spiritual path and felt that Mum would rather die at home. My sister could see that this might be a good thing but I had to do a huge job on persuading my brother, then to persuade the doctor to release Mum… not an easy task. Then I had to get the ambulance. This was not an easy task as all the health care workers were not at all used to doing a terminal journey in this way. With Mum on the stretcher and me in the ambulance beside her we set off for home. I talked to Mum all the way. As soon as Mum was carried into the house her eyes slowly opened. She turned a corner. Now my sister took over to train some girls to care for

Mum. I have not had children and thus found this intimate care of my mother difficult in a way that it had not been with Fred. My sister then returned to England to her husband and five children.

It was soon evident that Mum could not stay at her home alone in her present physical condition. A very small nursing home was found three hundred miles away. At this point Mum was not able to participate in the discussions as she was slowly coming back from death's door. Normally Mum would not consider any of us making a decision for her so we all found it difficult to be in the position to have to do this. My brother drove my mother and myself to this extra care nursing home accompanied by Mum's elderly dog. I stayed with Mum at the home for ten days to help her settle in and get comfortable with her routine. She was the only resident and it was wonderful that she was allowed to have her dog, which slept in her room beside her bed. That made a huge difference in her recovery. As she became stronger, it gave her a sense of purpose in making sure the dog was fed and walked. Mum had her 90th birthday at this place and she spent about nine months in this convalescent home.

Arriving back in the States I found that I had lost my job. Very understandable as this was the third extended compassionate break to assist Mum that I had had in a few years.

When Mum was stronger and able to start taking care of herself again, my sister came out and took Mum back home plus found a housekeeper/ nurse to stay with Mum. The problem was that Mum did feel better and found this housekeeper/

nurse not to be the sort of companion she wanted around, so it was not long before the housekeeper resigned.

Mum was simply not capable of running the house and there was no other choice than to get Mum into another nursing home with more of a sense of community. I could not come as I was looking for a job and my sister could not leave her family again, so my brother took on this particular challenge.

Mum was always consulted on our decisions about her health care. Sometimes Mum had an opinion while at other times just said 'do whatever you feel best.' And, sometimes what she said at one time would be the opposite the next time. I know the move would have been easier for Mum if I had been able to come and help, as there was much unhappiness surrounding the move and packing up her home.

The Elderly Care Facility to which Mum moved is one I had visited, on Mum's behalf, a few years previously. Mum had wanted my opinion because she recognized that she might have to go there. On that visit I was in tears about how depressing it was with its black security bars (thankfully now painted green). I do not know what I thought a 'home for the elderly' would be like.... This was not it.

However, as it turns out it is without question the best home for the Elderly in Kenya. It was a miracle that a room was available at the time Mum had to move.

Mum was very much a part of deciding what furniture to take to make her room her own. She recognized that she really had no alternative. She certainly did not want to go to England or to join me in the States for that matter. It must have been very sad for Mum to move from her huge garden and comfortable house to this small room with a tiny verandah just big enough for her wheelchair. Mum did not dwell on any of this, instead she would speak of how grateful she was that her room opened out onto a communal lawn where she could feed the birds just outside her room and that she was not a burden on her off spring. It was a warm and welcoming room.

For six years I visited Mum for my two weeks holiday, always staying with one of the other residents who had her own cottage in the compound. Thus I became part of the community and recognized its value. It was the right decision for Mum to move to this Home for the Elderly and the move actually gave Mum a continued sense of independence in that she was not beholden to any of her offspring. Taken as a whole this was the right decision for her and us, although it does seem sad that her care was in the hands of professionals and not family.

Mum accepted her increasing immobility and her aging with enormous dignity. It must have been immensely challenging after the busy life that she had led to be bedridden and to have failing eyesight and thus not to be able to read or write. Mum continued to be interested in her visitors – who were many of all ages even in the nursing home. Respecting her example I find myself being more and more interested in those around me. I enjoy friends both old and new and hope they find our time together to be as meaningful as I do.

Mum witnessed the blossoming of my new relationship with an important old boyfriend from the late 60s. The first time I brought him to see her in the nursing home she reminisced of occasions we were together in the past and had a wonderful twinkle in her eye. She could remember details I could not! This union definitely had her blessing for, on one of the last times that we visited Mum together, Mum said to Roger "Take care of my little girl" – and that he is doing.

I was immensely grateful that Mum showed her approval of this union with Roger in this way and very happy that Roger took it the way Mum meant. Of course I am not used to anyone taking care of me. I had been the breadwinner in the States and have made my own decisions about where I go and so on, so this idea of anyone taking care of me seemed very nurturing, especially when it is sad to have to say Mum was never able to do that herself. My sister and I were anything but nurtured. Of course, I may well read far too much into this request of Roger, however, it did feel as if it was an acknowledgement of the fact that Mum had not done that and now wanted to make sure that I be looked after.

Mum had a picture of Dad facing her bed in the small room in the nursing home. It was fading and in a disintegrating old leather frame. One day while looking towards this old sepia photograph, for she could no longer actually see the picture, Mum mused that she had now been widowed longer than she had been married to Dad. Dad died in 1967 when

Mum was 62 and he 75. There was great sadness, but not self pity, in this reflection. I could feel so deeply her loneliness and longing for Dad. And yet, I who was now also widowed at 57 felt both guilty and grateful to be embarking on a new relationship myself. I asked Mum if she felt Dad was waiting for her.... she did not know. Twice in the week before Mum died, though, Mum mentioned that she felt she had died the day Dad died. It is with enormous regret that I did not ask what that meant and what that felt like.

In fact I have my own sadness that I was not able to be with Mum as much as I would have liked in those last weeks. I visited Mum every day after work but the visits always felt rushed. We only had leisurely visits on the weekends. Mum was so clear she was ready to die and indeed was dying which is the reason she wanted me back in Kenya. Yet, somehow I could not actually accept that her time was so near the end. I could not seem to see her as a person fading away but still as the strong woman she had always been. In my rational mind I understood Mum was dying. In my heart, though, I could not seem to prepare for Mum's actual death. Mum, herself, was clear enough about the process. I still find this puzzling.

Mum had great wisdom and spoke of appropriate regrets for opportunities either not taken or not available, but never with any sense of the martyr. We were discussing death on one occasion and I asked her if she had any fears – her response was "Yes, I fear everlasting life – I do not want to be bored indefinitely." I thought about this for many months and asked friends how they would have responded. It was typical of Mum to see things differently from the norm; and, when she had a mind to, she would throw out questions or statements to challenge one intellectually. Mum's wisdom, unique perspectives and intellectual challenges continue to flow through me on more than one occasion.

May in Kenya is normally the long rains and these can be heavy. Indeed two nights before Mum died the rain had been so heavy that our whole drive was washed away and I could not get my car out. I had to walk to work and by evening Roger had managed to get our four-wheel drive vehicle out the driveway. Roger picked me up from work and took me straight over to see Mum. We were not able to stay long as we had no electricity at home and did not want to be out after dark. It was one of my briefest visits and it was one when Mum said she thought she had died. My mind was on Roger sitting in the car and of all the challenges we had at home. I am sad about missing that opportunity to talk.

At 6:20 the next morning there was a call on my mobile to say that Mum had died. The previous night Roger had left the car outside the drive so we were able to walk to it. We were at the nursing home soon after 7:00 am. Mum did not like one of her nurses who was due to come on duty at 7:00 so she had asked the gentle night nurse to bath her early before the other nurse came on duty. This was not normal and she had never done this before. She died soon after she was in her clean dress. And it was in this colorful dress covered by a white shroud that she was cremated.

I am so grateful for the time that Roger and I sat beside Mum quietly in her room until the mortuary people came to get her. I did not like seeing Mum being put into the black bag. Too recently I had seen a similar black bag as they took Fred away. In both instances I found the experience of strangers taking away my loved ones in those shiny cold black bags to be terribly difficult and strangely it even felt cruel. Roger and I packed up Mum's room and took everything home into our garage – and so within a few hours of Mum's death the room was clear.

Mum wanted to be cremated at the Hindu Crematorium and her ashes buried in Dad's grave. Mum was laid gently on a bed of very dry wood. She was not in a coffin. My sister and I together lit the shavings underneath the pyre and Mum's final wish was honored. After the memorial service we drove up to the church at Limuru and buried Mum's ashes on Dad's grave … just as Mum had wanted.

Now I am asked, "Are you Mavis Buxton's daughter?" In the years since Dad's death Mum has become valued in her own right. I will hear this sort of remark "What a wonderful old lady" and then some special memory of her – most often connected with horses or gardening. I can now smile and feel my heart sing in gratitude.

I still feel part of the community at the home for the elderly. I do some volunteer work for the home and visit my elderly friends there as often as I can.

Now I can feel in my core that Mum did know that it would be right for me to return to my roots in

Kenya for there is no doubt that I do feel as if I have come home. So in the end Mum did nurture me in her own way by creating the situation where I came back … to be with her when she died. To meet Roger again could not have been anticipated as none of us had been in contact. This was an added bonus, which has made it possible for me to stay here, with Mum's blessing.

At this moment it is a strange feeling to be writing about my mother with such deep affection and gratitude knowing that this is the end of my lineage. I have not had children and thus will not know what it is like to be a mother and to have a child remember me as their mother. I do know however what it is like to be a child and remember my mother. I cherish this.

NINE

There is Always Hope

Arianna

For about three years before my mother's death at the age of 84, she became increasingly forgetful from Alzheimer's Disease. This became an increasing gift, as she could no longer remember why she was angry. The days of difficulty picking a mother's day card expressing gratitude, fearing intimacy and respect were over. Frustrations did not escalate because all that was needed was changing the subject of discussion. The love/hate dance with an angel, the fun loving "life of the picnic" who could change into a shrill shirker ruining a holiday dinner at the drop of an eyelash was over. Her heartfelt joy at seeing me when I walked through the door made my visits to the nursing home a true gift. Helping her and my older sister (ten years older, mentally handicapped and living at home) became not so much a chore, but in more and more ways fun. In many ways we had become the family I had longed for – not perfect but joyous with being together.

New Respect for Mother

New respect and admiration for my mother began to emerge during these last years of her life. Even though she had constant hip pain from arthritis plus a failing memory, she was amazing. All her life she was frugal and spent very little on herself. Instead she helped each of her three daughters and her granddaughter. She was still driving two years before her death.

During this time my older sister suffered a psychotic depression and was hospitalized for a month. Mother drove herself to the hospital every day during the winter to visit her. Pittsburgh in winter is very challenging to drive through even for the experienced driver. My younger sister and I lived one hundred miles away and could only help out on weekends. Mother was there for my older sister even in the snow. Once a passerby in the parking lot of the hospital helped her clean the snow off her car in the dark after visiting hours were over so she could get into her car. Her love and desire to take care of her daughters was so evident not even snow storms would prevent her from being with the one that needed help.

Perhaps mother was reliving the major depression she experienced when pregnant with this first child. The birth was traumatic, and the child was later found to have slight mental retardation. Never again would mother have another major mental illness, yet the underlying tension with not having her emotional life straight was an underlying theme running through our family life.

Certainly being the seventh child of Russian immigrants proved to serve her well. Her family was quite resourceful. They were able to pay cash for a humble yet roomy house with a large garden. This fed them and many in the neighborhood during the depression. Like their neighbors, they attended the Orthodox Russian Church and lived in an ethnic community. With no savings and no debt, the depression was not as hard on them as many who lost more. In my life I am discovering these same traits well ingrained and giving me strength, resourcefulness and a keen sense of finances.

Dedication to Family

Family was highly regarded by my mother. Her own mother died at home of some pulmonary problem, perhaps TB after lingering for months. Her last word was calling my mother's name. At fifteen years of age Mother was motherless. She continued to live briefly with a father who had a drinking problem plus two older brothers. Quitting high school, which was common at that time, she went to work. Soon she moved in with her older sister who was newly married. It was decided that living with her father and brothers might be dangerous for a young and beautiful woman. One wonders how welcome she felt with the newlyweds. This shifting of her family constellation seemed to impress on Mother the importance of her own family and instilled the dedication to stay together and help her daughters in every way. Her need to belong and have a permanent place in her family was very strong.

Father developed Crohn's Disease, a very painful inflammation of the colon that was constantly misdiagnosed. My mother's memories of her early marriage were ones of silence as he struggled with long spells on the toilet. She was determined to love and support Father during this time just like she did with her mother. Duty to family was of major importance to her. And I find myself expressing this duty to family as an underlying theme of my life also.

Family life improved after surgeries removed the diseased parts of Father's colon. Then ten years later I was born. Then ten years after that, my baby sister was born, a surprise but very wanted.

This dedication to family was warmed by the love and caring between my parents. My mother was repeatedly a lifesaver in helping my father receive the correct diagnosis and treatment for his illness. Taking him on a train to the Mayo Clinic when he was quite weak was a real feat requiring much patience. Yet, her temper and lack of ability to hold her tongue were a frequent vexation. As my younger sister and I became teens it was made worse by her accusations of our morality and "what exactly we had let our boyfriends do."

Father had migraine headaches and began using Valium at increasing prescribed doses. Whenever Mother felt sufficiently crossed by father or anyone, she would threaten to have another breakdown. I once overheard her trump card, when she blamed my father for the lack of appropriate medical care that resulted in the mental retardation of my older sister.

Father died at 61, frail and worn from the numerous medical issues that caught up with him. I know he was relieved and could not blame him.

Mother's dedication to family and determination to keep the family together were quite evident even months prior to mother's death. While she was still living at home, I was visiting at her home. Around midnight we were still up talking and enjoying our time together. My older sister suddenly stood up and said she had to go to the bathroom. She walks a little slow but tried to rush to avoid having an accident, tripped and fell. When she fell, my 300 pound 60 year old sister had massive diarrhea.

She could not get up and was literally covered with poop from her waist to her feet. My mother and I had her crawl to the bathroom and edged her up on the toilet. I wondered how in the world we were going to clean her up. Being a nurse I had cleaned up patients before, even so, the amount of dirtiness was overwhelming. My mother had the love and dedication to literally push me out the door and said that she would take care of it. She did so cheerfully, not blaming my sister for this accident.

I did not insist on helping because her sense of pride in taking care of her child needed to be respected. Perhaps she did not want to scare me in the duty I had claimed in being the caretaker of my sister after her passing. Mother gave my sister a sponge bath. When done my sister was cleaner than if she would have had a shower. It took an hour; mother finished around 1:00 a.m. The incredible strength of her love for her children, both my sister and I, really shone brightly that night. I felt proud of her accomplishment with a new respect and gratitude for her. The deep hurt of her temper from earlier years was being replaced by an increasing sense of gratitude which has made me much more aware of the larger picture in so many situations.

Independent Living

In the last years of her life, I tried to convince my mom to sell her house and move to a senior apartment complex less than a mile from me. The 100 miles between us was becoming more and more of a burden as her health deteriorated and I had to be there more and more. She always refused saying she wanted to die in her home. Who could blame her? My parents had built their dream home over 40 years ago. Dad fulfilled his dream of being an architect when he designed the house on their kitchen table. Mom wanted a fireplace and ceramic tile above the kitchen counter so she sold Avon to earn the money for the improvements to the plan. As a teenager her experience at GC Murphy's cosmetic counter plus summer modeling in the store window certainly came full circle to support her in building their dream home. After 20 + years since my father's passing, their romance grew larger and larger in Mother's recollection. The troubles they had in their marriage were forgotten, but the love that went into their dream home sustained her for the rest of her life. I so value my independence and have finally found my dream home, which I plan to live in the rest of my life.

The Last Thanksgiving

Arriving for Thanksgiving I was alarmed to see a large amount of swelling in Mother's legs that was not there two weeks earlier. I knew she needed to go to the hospital for treatment, but felt she could last one more night before taking her to a hospital near me. That Thanksgiving dinner no one rushed. No one sprung up to get the dishes going. We all lingered, sensing that this may be the last Thanksgiving together. We savored the love and the sense of my father's presence at the dinner. Mother was told that in the morning she would come with me and I would take her to a doctor to get "checked out." Later that evening she was looking for some money to put in her purse and was concerned that she thought she was broke.

In the last year or so, she forgot about her large bank accounts and the cash she hid in the house. Wanting to help her get ready, I got out a large stash of bills from a hiding place that she had forgotten. As far as she knew, this was all the money she had in the world. She would not believe me when I would show her the bank statement reflecting a large amount of money. She was delighted and began counting the cash over and over since she would loose track. I was a bit afraid of where she might hide it next. It seemed there was about $2,000. Placing a 20 and a few ones in her wallet, she then divided up the rest, giving it to my sisters, her only granddaughter and me.

So the last night in her home, she gave it all (in her mind) away. This is how much she loved us, with giving her all. This makes me feel cherished and grateful. There is comfort in the fact that she never had another home, and in that sense, died there as she wished.

The remaining 4 months of her life were spent in one hospital after another. She only had 4 days at my home between Nov 27th and the day she died on Feb 13th.

Reversal of Roles

With mother's downhill slide the last 4 months of her life the reversal of roles became more pronounced. She had pulmonary emboli, complicated by pulmonary hypertension and an upper respiratory infection. All of these required increasing physical care. I found myself in a very loving place to give to her just a small piece of the love that she had given to me. I was beginning to understand love from a whole new perspective.

After she died, I realize that I grieved for the mother who gave me birth and loved and cared for the infant and toddler, as well as for the innocent love of a child that she gave me in the last years of her life. I miss my responsibility as well as the open heart that connected us that last year and at the time of her death. The most heartfelt tears to my eyes are ones similar to loosing a child. Paradoxically, I can also feel the love of her mature strength and commitment to our family.

Good Times

In my mother's last few months she would say I was her sister. Once she asked how she knew me. I could not be horrified at that question because her glee was so innocent when she was reminded I was her daughter. She said "I always liked you. Now I know you are my daughter, too!" Her beaming smile at this new discovery made me happy too. In a way, these were good times. I enjoyed the role of hero to the family and all the unconditional love. Even more I was really hungry for the unconditional love that I had not experienced as a child. I was filling my cup until it ran over with love. There is now plenty to share with family and friends.

Death where is thy Sting?

The night Mother died, I was there with my two closest girlfriends. Mother was in a step down intensive care bed. Due to her long course of illness and poor prognosis, she was made a "Do Not Resuscitate." Although she had not spoken in the last week, she could still squeeze my hand two days before her passing. The last night she was not responding.

We knew of her imminent death and said our good byes with hugs and let her know that it was okay to go. We prayed over her and surrounded her with light and called in the angels and her family who had passed. We chatted at her bedside about my plans for the future and how my older sister (who was then staying with me) and I would go on. It was enjoyable as there was a sense of relief for my mother as well as for everyone. There was continuity in family life. Everything was being taken care of for her.

One of my girlfriends is psychic and said she could see that my mother was already out of her body, and sitting with us enjoying the conversation. My girlfriend said my father turned up and said it was time to go but mother wanted to stay a while longer. I think to find out what I was going to do. My friend said that my mother and father each put a hand on my shoulder and said how proud they were of me and how much they loved me. That made me cry with love and joy because I knew it was true.

When we decided to go to the ladies room Mother left with Dad. The nurse ran down the hall to say that she was taking her last breath. Afterwards we helped select what mother would wear out of the hospital and gathered up her things. My girlfriends were not in a hurry to leave rather choosing to linger in the atmosphere of love and help with the final tasks. By this time it was probably 2:00 a.m. They both later thanked me for the incredible gift of spirit and awareness they received at Mom's passing. The dying seemed to give us more than we gave her. It was a special blessing that if you are lucky, you will receive from a loved one.

Postscript

Being in a love/hate tug of war with Mother most of my life, these last years together were very healing. This was an incredible gift to expand the love and release the hate. We healed and began to relate in ways that could not otherwise occur except in mother's final stage of life.

I am submitting my story anonymously to help those of you who are going through a trying time with a difficult mother. I learned that there is always hope, that the pure intention of a mother's love will shine through.

On my father's deathbed twenty-two years prior, I promised that we would go on as a family if he had to leave. I think that promise was kept. Now this promise is extended to my mother. I now have a new child - my older sister. This has also been a joyful duty. Being on a mission of love brings great meaning and purpose. As our family goes on, so does the love.

TEN

Growing in Grace

Helen Martin

How does one distill the countless gifts of a lifetime from a mother to her child? Perhaps some of the most outstanding gifts that my Mother gave to me include her faithful instruction to love God and serve Him, her consistent example as a virtuous woman and her love for me - thus teaching me about God's love. Mother taught me "Every good gift and every perfect gift is from above, and comes down from the Father." (James 1:17) As I consider what gifts Mother gave to me, I must give God all the glory for those gifts. Mother would have it no other way. God must always receive all glory in all things.

Cancer was what took Mother's earthly body – but not her eternal soul. It was only four months after Daddy, at age 81, had gone to be with the Lord.

Mother had loved Daddy faithfully for over forty-five years. When Mother and Daddy moved to the farm from town in 1952 it was very difficult for her. She helped Daddy and learned to do many chores in and around the barn, which were arduous and dirty. Yet, she loved Daddy very much and even though farm life was hard for her, she did her best to help him. When Daddy was dying, it was Mother who took care of him. We now know she was very ill herself at the time, but she sacrificed her own comfort to ease his suffering. This selflessness was typical of her.

Moments after Daddy went to be with the Lord, Mother, who had loved God for over 55 years, began to weep. She said, "I'm not worthy. I get mad. I say mean things that I wish I had never said. I hurt people I love and care about. I'm not worthy." I began to weep and Tom, my brother, gently reminded Mother what she had taught us – that this is what God's grace was all about. God loved us while we were unworthy of His love and only if we understand our own unworthiness to come to God do we begin to know God. I nodded in agreement and held Mother's hand.

The Thursday before Easter 1990 after mother's surgery, at age 71, the doctor said very simply, "I will be surprised if she is alive in six months." The news was difficult to absorb.

Mother could not return to the farmhouse to live alone. My overwhelming concern was how to prepare my house so that when my mother came home from the hospital, she would have a comfortable place to live. My pastor's wife had asked me to call her after Mother's surgery. I placed the phone call and recounted what the doctor had told me. She responded, "I will rally the troops!"

God provided all the help to prepare my house and a bedroom for Mother to be ready Easter weekend. There must have been thirty-five people in and out of my house that Easter weekend as Mother was due home from the hospital on Tuesday. The first man arrived at 7:00 a.m. on Good Friday morning and many worked till late at night each day. One twelve year old painted the closet. The Young Singles Bible Study cleaned, painted, and moved furniture. We found a nightstand and a chair and rug that matched! Several senior citizens helped with cleaning and were at my home to accept a furniture delivery when I could not be at home. There were countless acts of God caring for Mother and me. God took care of all of the home preparations.

In the prior January, about a month after Daddy went to be with the Lord but before we knew that Mother was seriously ill, she expressed her desire to travel to England. She had always wanted to go and meet my many friends who live in England yet had never been able to travel there. We planned to leave at the beginning of July but when we learned how ill mother was, I wondered if she wanted to make the trip. I told Mother that it was her choice. If she wanted to go, I would be happy to take her. If she wanted to remain at home, I would be content to do that as well. Mother responded immediately, "I want to go to London."

We flew to London in mid June. I confess I believed that I would be flying home with a coffin and wondered how one would make such arrangements. God allowed Mother to have three weeks at a Holiday

Inn near Heathrow airport outside of London. While we were there, Mother was able to travel and see things perhaps four days in that three week period of time.

One Sunday afternoon I hired a driver to drive us around London as Mother was unable to handle public transport or even a tour bus. She enjoyed seeing St. Paul's Cathedral, the Houses of Parliament and Big Ben and especially enjoyed a visit to Elephant and Castle to see the location were the Baptist preacher Charles Haddon Spurgeon had preached 100 years earlier. Mother and Daddy had read his devotionals for years with their daily Bible readings. My favorite photo of that day was a picture I took of my Mother, Elizabeth, in front of Buckingham Palace. On another day, we visited Oxford where I had studied plus the village of Penn. Being from Pennsylvania, this was important to her. Another day we obtained a wheel chair and a friend and I took her to see Windsor Castle and Queen Mary's Doll House. While the outings were few Mother's daily delight was to walk down to the gift shop in the hotel and buy post cards to send to her family and countless friends.

One morning, while we were in England, mother lamented the fact that she could no longer sing. She told me that she was looking forward to Heaven when she would be able to sing God's praises. Mother loved music. She studied the piano for over twelve years and she sang in the choirs of various churches she attended over the years. In the last years of her life on Earth, her voice became weak and faltering yet her faith grew stronger and more unshakeable. As Mother became weaker, she never complained. She was delighted to be in England!

About a week after we returned home from the United Kingdom, I drove Mother to an oncologist's appointment scheduled before we went to England. The oncologist sent her to the Emergency Room and then came over to the ER himself. The oncologist was a jerk! He began to yell at me in the Emergency Room. "Why did you take your mother to England? You had no right to do that. You are trying to kill off your mother!" I began to cry and he began to chase me around the ER continuing to yell at me. I wanted him to leave me alone long enough for me to regain my composure so that I could tell him that my Mother made her own decisions and I believed that my role was to support her in what she wanted to do.

Mother was in the hospital for several weeks. When it was time to leave the hospital, I remembered that she had given me a very generous gift. Mother told me on three separate occasions when she was reasonably healthy that if the time came when I was unable to care for her, she would not mind if she went to a home where she could receive the care that she needed. I researched several options and discussed them with Mother and she chose to go to Harrison House. Mother received excellent, loving care at Harrison House. The oncologist was furious as he wanted to keep my mother as his patient and this move would mean that she was out of his territory. Mother wanted so much to be away from him. Mother's strength in choosing her own doctor by the simple act of moving into Harrison House reminded me there is often a gentle solution to a seemingly horrendous situation.

Mother was confident in what was right and wrong. One Sunday while she was at Harrison House, her 80-year old roommate, Ruthie, did not receive her usual small dish of ice cream, which was frequently given to each patient on Sundays with dinner. Ruthie eagerly looked forward to her ice cream once a week – she ALWAYS had ice cream on Sunday. This dish of ice cream had become the highlight of her week! On this particular Sunday, however, Ruthie was given pudding instead. She was devastated! Mother told her directly, "You stand up for your rights and go out there and tell them you want your ice cream!" Ruthie did just that and went out into the hall to the head nurse and said, "My roommate said to demand my rights. I would like my ice cream, please." She got her small dish of ice cream that day. I also went out and brought two boxes of ice cream for her to keep in the freezer in case there was an "ice cream shortage" another day.

About two months after that horrible incident in the emergency room with the oncologist, Mother had to return for a medical problem. While there, a nurse came up to me and said, "I remember you and your mother. You were here about two months ago. I will never forgive that doctor for the way he treated you that day." I repeated to the nurse the fact that Mother knew and understood what was happening and that she had made her own choices and I believed that it was my responsibility to support her and her choices. I felt vindicated after talking to that nurse that day.

Early the Sunday morning, just hours before she went to meet the Lord, I came home to shower and change after having been by her bedside for several days. When I returned, I found Mother's Bible open on her bed. One of the nurses at Harrison House had been reading Scripture to my Mother from her own Bible. Mother had been in great pain and the nurse had come in and seen Mother's Bible and opened it to where her marker was and read to her until she was able to settle down and rest more comfortably. I was blessed to learn how lovingly and respectfully they treated Mother, knowing that was a blessing from God.

In those last hours Tom and I were with Mother. Her breathing became more difficult and then she was with Christ the Savior. We were watching and waiting with her. "I think she is gone." "I think you are right." I went out to tell the nurse. I felt we needed to stay with Mother's earthly body until someone came to take her. My emotions were mixed. I felt happy she wasn't suffering any more and was in the presence of God worshiping Him and singing His praises and yet I was sad that she was separated from me.

Interestingly General Stonewall Jackson's doctor told him on May 10, 1863 that he would die before the day was over. Jackson was a very godly man and he responded, "It is the Lord's Day, my wish is fulfilled. I have always desired to die on Sunday." Like Jackson, Mother went to be with the Lord on a Sunday at 11:50 p.m.

Shortly before Mother went to be with the Lord, I had ordered an upholstered recliner chair for my home. The store called on the Monday after Mother went to be with the Lord and said that the chair had arrived but not with the trim I had ordered. They offered to sell the chair to me at cost. I agreed and the chair was delivered the day before Mother's Memorial Service. The deliveryman gave me a single red rose and said that it was the store's policy to give their customers a single red rose.

Immediately I recalled a story that Mother had told me years before of her very first memory. When Mother was three years old she was in her mother's arms being carried away from a rapidly approaching train. Her mother was struck and killed by that train. When the conductor went looking for my mother, he found the small child between the tracks under the train! Mother's leg was severely cut. She was in the hospital and then a nursing home for a very long time. Her earliest memory was a man she did not know - a total stranger - handing to her a single red rose while she was recovering from that injury.

Here were the bookends of her virtuous life – a life typified by acts of God providing for Mother's needs and caring for her throughout her entire life. Mother had a loving mother who sacrificed her life for her daughter. Mother had a loving father who went to be with the Lord months before she married her life-long husband. Mother had two children who cared for her and watched over her with love. Mother had nurses who loved and cared for her at Harrison House in her last days here on Earth. When family was not around her providing for her needs, God provided friends and even strangers to meet her needs her entire life. God provides for all of us.

The closer Mother was to her death, the more godly she became. Through all the pain, even as she got weaker and weaker, Mother was confident and strong in the salvation of God and often said "there is no condemnation to those who are in Christ Jesus." She lived by example. Her life was a life of growing in grace and godliness. I thank God for my mother and the example of virtue she gave to me.

What is virtue? It is not perfection but it is growth in grace in one who loves God. Virtue is seen because God creates, God protects and God preserves. In the Bible, Proverbs chapter 31 notes the great value of a virtuous woman. Proverbs notes that the heart of her husband safely trusts in her, and her children rise up and call her blessed. Elizabeth Temple Walker Martin was a virtuous woman on earth, she entered into the Lord's presence on the day we celebrate the resurrection – Sunday. Today she is with the Master, singing His praises with a voice more beautiful than she ever had on earth. Her example of godliness and her consistent urging of her children, family and friends to have faith in God was the greatest gift a mother could give her child.

God gave Mother life, protected Mother's life and provided wonderful people to care for her all of her days. Mother learned of God's love from her earliest days and as she learned more, she trusted more. Mother knew that each gift came from God. She taught her children to study God's Word and encouraged all her family and friends to read the Bible and to seek to know God. These gifts are her great legacy to her children, family and friends. Each day as I grow in wisdom and understanding, I thank God for the gifts He gave me through my mother.

ELEVEN

Mother Lost and Found

Jayne E. Andron

I can't believe she's dead! It's been a year as I'm writing this. My mother's death was sudden and unexpected after six years in a nursing home suffering the progressive effects of Alzheimer's Disease. Her slow regression and slipping-away from reality was over.

There are trite sayings about Alzheimer's. The one I find most meaningful is "long goodbye" which is described as losing a loved one in increments. The truth is that it begins without prelude or warning and is so subtle that one can mistake the signs. I lived nearly 1000 miles from my parents; and, as I only saw them a couple of times a year, was unaware of the little changes that Dad chalked up to moodiness.

My first recognition of Mother's decline began by her telling the same story over and over when we were talking by phone or asking the same question several times within a few minutes. At first I thought she was just not listening and I became very irritated with her. When my parents came for a visit they had scarcely arrived before Mother began asking when they would return home. Mother couldn't remember from one moment to the next if we'd planned to go out for dinner or were going to a movie.

The little things were the first almost unrecognizable signs. She constantly harped on the same subject telling the same story obsessively. It was then that a neighbor, who is a nurse, first suggested to me that there was something neurological involved in Mom's behavior. I realized there was more going on than just "bad" behavior. Within a year Mom no longer recognized my voice when I called her and soon didn't know who I was if she didn't see my face.

The first time she ended a phone conversation by politely thanking me for my call, I cried with the pain of a child who has lost her mother in a crowd. There was a feeling of being distanced from her with no way of reconnecting. I felt lost. And this was only the beginning.

However, there was a flip side to this period of fuzzy thinking. Mom had always been a reserved, polite, almost-regal Southern Belle. She never left the house without her hair and makeup perfectly in place and was self-conscious about her appearance. With the memory loss there also came liberation from the constraints of politeness. She laughed louder, felt more relaxed, and lost her obsession with her health. It was as if she were freed from a life-long concern with appropriateness. It was a delight to see her so comfortable with herself. But sadly she continued to decline until there was no choice but to place her in a care facility. At this point it had been almost six years since I first noticed the changes in her personality, and she would live for another six years at Hidden Acres Nursing Facility. It was a long goodbye, and I did lose my mother in increments.

I was prepared for her death, I even prayed for it at times; and then, that final Christmas I prayed that she would hold on for just one more holiday. When the call came on January 7 that she was dying, I entered a mind-numbing state of shock. As I rushed home from work to pack and fly to be at her side, all I could think was "please hold on, please, Mom." I hoped that she would make it for a couple more hours until I could be with her. My desire for these many years had always been to be present when she died.

Mother couldn't wait that long. Around 2:00 p.m. as I was flying from Philadelphia, Pennsylvania to Nashville, Tennessee, I awoke from a nap with a sudden "knowing" that Mother was gone. I sensed a tingling energy surrounding me as we flew through the clouds. As I peered out the window of the plane at 35,000 feet I felt that those clouds were intermingled with her energy, that finally my mother was free of her burdensome body and was pure, unencumbered, joyful Light. Finally, after all these years, she was soaring and at peace. Honest to God, that's how I felt in an instant upon awakening. I closed my eyes and cried to relieve the pressure of sadness and loss that sat in my chest surrounding my heart.

Arriving in Nashville an hour later I placed a phone call to my sister who confirmed that Mom had died at the time I awoke sensing her joyous release. My Dad, brother, and sister were with her when she opened her eyes for the last time. For the first time in many months Mother made eye contact with each of them. Later, as Daddy sat by her side, she slipped away quietly, alone with the man who had shared her life for almost 60 years. My siblings and I knew that was the way her death should be.

I was all right with not being present at her death. I was immensely gratified with the "fly-by", a connection with Spirit at the time of death. Her illness had taken Mom away from me in small baby steps. I hadn't had a connection with her in many years. I felt then, as I feel now, that the release from her body allowed for the possibility for communion and connection on another level. I call it a spiritual level for lack of a better term but I think that it is the universal field that connects everything and I only began to explore this information in response to mother's death. The periodic closeness I felt to Mom after her body was gone was so incredible to me. It confirmed for me not just the continuity of life but also my belief in the oneness of all things.

At first I could not believe that Mary Vernon Judkins Emmitt no longer existed on Earth. How could she not BE here anymore? My mind hadn't caught up with what my intuition had sensed immediately upon her dying. Many times I have questioned if we can intuit things, sense them and feel the emotions, long before our brain can process the physical reality. As my consciousness awoke to my mother's death, it certainly appeared that way to me. I had responded emotionally with sadness and tears hours before the fact of the event was communicated to me. Such a profound realization: there is no separation. Everything is known immediately on the intuit level. Not even words are needed.

For several weeks afterward I still had moments when my mind told me that it was incomprehensible that my mother did not exist in this world. Even though she was not able to connect with me, Mom had always been present in my life. I lived near her for the last two-and-a-half years of her life and visited several times a week. I went to see her when I was sad and wanted to feel her touch, or when she needed me to be there to help her eat or to calm her down; it didn't matter that she couldn't relate to me, that she didn't know who I was or appreciate my concern and care for her. I knew; and I was doing it for me so I could continue to have a relationship my mother, so I would have no regrets, and that relationship was enough for me.

I remember so well her last cognitive connection with me. We were standing in her room at Hidden Acres watching a brilliant sunset, the first time she had connected with anything outside herself in a very long time. Feeling close to her in that moment, I put my arm around her shoulders. She turned to me, making eye contact and took my face in her hands. "I always only wanted the very best for you," she said. Then she "went away" again, not able to see neither me nor the sunset, as she had been doing for many months.

I wanted more time to tell her what I had always wanted for her but she was gone again. I didn't have the time, but I had those words from her with all she meant to convey and I could bring that warm feeling back by being present with her. Now I no longer had a mother in this world and it didn't seem right that the Earth could continue to spin without her on it.

After she died, mother communicated with me emotionally through experiences that were very real to me throughout the rest of that winter and spring.

The first experience occurred when I was driving back to Pennsylvania the week after her memorial service. Heading northeast through Virginia very early in the morning the sky was lightening with a soft golden glow. Clouds began to appear like spirals and trails in the sky. With each minute and mile that passed the trails became more brilliant and spiraled higher and higher. I found out later that these are called contrails, but at that moment I had never seen such a magnificent display. A strong impression came to me that Mom was among the clouds "dancing" higher and higher with her newfound freedom. I felt joyful and wished I had a camera to capture that morning, that impression forever. I wanted a picture that would bring this moment clearly to memory.

Arriving home late that night, I opened a card that had arrived from a friend who as a young girl had lost her mother to cancer. She expressed her sympathy for the loss that I was experiencing. The front of the card was a picture of a milder version of the sky I had seen that morning. I felt the same joyful sensation as I pulled it from the envelope. I laughed out loud and said, "Thanks for the picture, Mom!"

I continue to discover that even the picture cannot bring back the true experience. But, I can be in that moment and feel that connectedness, that Presence with such intensity that the actual picture isn't needed. The formless feeling of joy is far stronger.

During that winter following my mother's death, my best friend, Cindy, was experiencing the decline of her mother's health. Lilianne had a recurrence of breast cancer that had metastasized to the neck and brainstem. By April Lilianne had chosen to discontinue treatment and go into hospice care. The prognosis was for 6-8 weeks in which she chose to be in her own home surrounded with her family.

I felt so sad for Cindy. She and her mother were close in ways my mother and I weren't. This loss was going to be painful for Cindy and would impact her on a day-to-day basis.

Lilianne had been so kind to me after my mother's diagnosis. Each time I saw her she would clasp me to her and say, "You need a Mommy Hug." Her hugs represented the closeness that I missed and allowed me, for a moment, to feel safe and loved. I cherished those "Mommy" hugs as well as the woman who offered them.

A few days before Cindy and I were going to visit Lilianne, I was in the process of ironing a tablecloth for lunch with Cindy and our friend Jane. Ironing has always been a meditative experience for me. Out of the blue I was overwhelmed by the thought of my mother. I began talking to her out loud, telling her that she was going to meet Lilianne soon. I remembered and spoke to Mom about how they both had brothers that had died before them and, oh, what a wonderful reunion they would have. Again, thinking of my mother gave me a feeling of great peace and joyousness.

About half an hour later, Jane arrived. I could tell immediately that something was "up" because she wasn't her usual chipper self. A number of things flitted through my mind as I asked her what was wrong. "I hate to be the bearer of bad news," she answered, "but Lilianne died this morning - about 30 minutes ago."

My immediate reaction was, "Oh, my God" as tears welled and I felt my heart fill with the heaviness of this loss, then I felt shivers up my body. My next reaction was to tell Jane that my mother had "told me" earlier. Perhaps by giving me the image of a reunion with her own brother Mom had passed along the awareness that Lilianne had passed over and was reunited with her own brother. I felt sadness for the death of my friend's mom and I also felt a deep peaceful connection to both our mothers.

Later I wondered why Mom would be so emphatic and clear in passing that information to me. Perhaps she was present at the arrival of the woman who had given "Mommy Hugs" to the daughter whom she had forgotten in the last years of her increasing dementia. I felt the strength and permanence of "mother-love" in that experience. It emboldens and strengthens me yet. I am stronger because of those two women and the wisdom they imparted through the experiences of their deaths as well as by their lives.

I remain always amazed at the ways and times I've felt my mother's presence since her death. While she lived in her altered state of Alzheimer's dementia, I didn't feel a connection to her in this way. I don't have this sense of her presence often. When I do it occurs at a significant time or event.

I am a Bereavement Counselor with a hospice in the Philadelphia area. The first time following mother's death that I co-led a Memorial Service I realized and finally understood that although I had prepared for mother's death for many years, I was not prepared for her loss. Loss is the beginning of another journey following the death of a loved one and there is no way to prepare for it. It is an experience all its own. The process following a death is learning to live with the empty spot that is left and yet not letting that loss define ones life from that point on forever. Just as my mother's illness was a learning experience, her death initiated a new journey into the experience of living with loss.

Loss is the experience on the other side of death including the rituals surrounding it. We begin by giving and receiving comfort from one another, by sharing in some form of ceremony whether it is a funeral service or a memorial dinner party. It is a new journey and we begin walking through it at Ground Zero. There is no way around, over, or under this path; each one of us must walk through loss one step at a time with all the feelings that accompany us: pain of never seeing that person again, joy at remembrance of the life we shared, anger at being left with the detritus of a life left behind, relief at physical pain now ended, or regret for things left undone or unsaid. As each experience of loss is colored by the nature of one's relationship with the deceased, each experience is unique. I've found that the death of my mother is wholly my own experience. I'm not even experiencing this loss in the same way I've gone through other deaths.

Often, in my counseling, I find that I don't relate to the experiences of mother-loss in the same way as some other women. My mother was not my best friend and confidante. We didn't have the opportunity to spend a lot of time together; in fact, we seldom lived within a thousand miles of each other after I left for college. I always felt that there was potential for us to have a closer relationship; we had moved closer to each other after she was diagnosed with a mind-altering illness but we never had the chance to fulfill my fantasies of an adult mother-daughter friendship.

My main feeling of sadness is the loss of potential, of possibility. Lost potential. I may not miss her in my daily routine or when I want a sounding board, but my heart aches at the awareness of the void surrounding her absence at those times when I do want her nearby. I'm disappointed that she didn't see her grandsons' graduations or know their career choices. She didn't know that I got a Master's degree. She didn't see me the first time I wore a "power suit" to make a presentation at an End-of-Life Conference. I missed her presence at those and many other events. At the same time I know that I am a strong woman because of her belief in me and I am aware of how proud she would be if she were physically here to see who I am today.

Finally I appreciate and realize that my mother is still teaching me and giving me gifts. Her illness and decline caused me to be more compassionate. Her death provided the opportunity to experience her presence on a different plane. Her loss guides me each day as I do the work of a bereavement professional. Her love for me transcends time and space, enlarges my capacity for caring, and enables me to understand the universal pain of loss. Although I have lost my mother physically, I have a new relationship with her. I have found a new strength, a deeper awareness of who I am and the gifts I have to offer others.

Mother, I thank you for the gift of life and for the gifts you left behind in your death.

TWELVE

Permission to Die and Fear of Death

Bozena M. Padykula

Facing my fear of death has been the most significant event not only in my nursing experience but in my life. And, giving my mother permission to die in my home was the most life-affirming gift she could have given me.

Death was the one aspect of nursing care that paralyzed my brain and escalated my fears as a student nurse. I was scared of witnessing a death as a student nurse because I did not know what was expected of me when someone is taking the last breath. My first image of death was it would be something tragic, loud and the person would keep telling me how it felt. Throughout my nursing program, without any clinical background, I pictured my first patient dying in the hospital, and me probably fainting or calling for help. I imagined myself being numb, unresponsive and not knowing how to support the person's needs in that moment. My mind created an impressive scenario based on the unknown of the future.

To keep my fears at ease, I also imagined myself in a cardiac emergency where everybody around me knew what tasks to perform. My presence there was to only observe and support other staff. I thought that presence of other staff would diminish my fears. The more people around me, the better for me or so I thought. Deep in my heart I knew I had to face my fear by being present at someone's death, but on the other hand, I was not ready to face that experience. Sooner or later, I needed to be ready for that moment, put my fears aside and deal with the situation at hand.

The last thing that I expected in overcoming my fear of death was to give permission to my own mother to let go, to die. Based on the doctor's prognosis and the course of my mother's disease, her death was inevitable. I did not believe it would come as soon as it did. I believed in miracles or something that would heal her or make her physically well again. She fought colon cancer for 3 ½ years. Based on her initial diagnosis, she was given less than a year to live.

During numerous courses of her treatment, her strong will to live kept her going and did not allow her to give up hope. Her determination to stay independent kept her active almost to the last day her life. I'm even more proud of her accomplishments because she managed to build so much independence in a new country.

When she came from Poland to the U.S.A. in 1991 at the age of 46 she didn't know the English language. She soon gained and treasured independence in all her daily activities, including work, shopping, cooking, and maintaining an apartment until she moved in with us in December of 1999. Throughout months of chemotherapy, radiation and numerous doctors' visits, she drove independently to each appointment. At times she faced a communication barrier due to her limited English language. As a result I would meet her at the doctor's office. Her continuous strength in facing obstacles in her life was giving me the role model and the strength to face my fear.

At age 50 Mom was diagnosed with colon cancer. She faced another tremendous change in her life - adjusting to a colostomy. Once she told me she thought moving to a new country would be the biggest hardship of her life. Mom felt unprepared to face any stronger hardships such as a diagnosis of colon cancer and adjustment to a colostomy. However, she learned how to maintain the colostomy quickly. Even living in my home she was determined to maintain the colostomy independently. Two days before she died was the first time I took over the care of her colostomy. She impressed me with how clean and organized she was when caring for her colostomy. A few times she shared with me her tips on how to make life with a colostomy more efficient during cleaning, changing bags, and emptying them. These tips became a great resource when I started caring for my first patient with a colostomy in the hospital setting. Now I share these tips with my nursing students during their clinical experiences.

After adjustment to life with a colostomy, she believed her cancer would be cured; and, this is what

I let her believe. The language barrier between the doctors and my mom allowed me to keep her true prognosis a secret from her. I was fully aware that all the medical measures were palliative. There was no chance to eradicate her cancer. But, since I lived in a state of denial coupled with a fear of death, I kept convincing her and myself that everything would be okay and the cancer would be eliminated from her body.

Over the years her disease progressed. When her condition declined to the level that she was not able to care for herself, I decided to take her into my home. Six months had passed since graduating from nursing school. Now Mom was moving in with my family for the last six months of her physical life. I started to realize her cancer would not evaporate and the end was approaching. When I first offered her to live with us she absolutely refused. She didn't want to disturb our family life plus she insisted that any nursing home would meet her needs. My family, however, opened their hearts to her and, with much reassurance, she agreed. We felt she would be loved, safe and our home was the most appropriate place for her at this time.

Strange, she did not mention even once that she would like to go back to her home in Poland, and the life she had with her husband. She and Dad were closely attached through frequent phone calls and his occasional yearly visits.

Deep in my heart I knew I had made the right decision by inviting her to our home. Even so I was so scared as to how my whole family would adjust to this change. Encouragement and support from my husband and my kids reassured me that there were no other options for my mom. I felt so proud of my family and their ability to give their love to Mom in this way.

Without even thinking what would be ahead of us, I believed that staying positive and adjusting to things as they arrived would keep my fears under control. I was not thinking neither how long nor how difficult caring for my mom would be. One thing that I wanted to handle was to adjust our house to her needs and to make the environment comfortable. I was pleased that we were able to provide a separate bedroom for my mom on the same floor with the rest of the bedrooms. Having her on the same floor during the night made us all feel more comfortable that in case of emergency we could quickly handle any difficult situation. As a result when her condition declined and she required oxygen, we were able to hear her difficult breathing when she removed the nasal canula. We could quickly put it back to help her breathing.

Another positive factor of her bedroom on the second floor was easy access to the bathroom. She was very meticulous about caring for her colostomy. The bathroom close to her bedroom provided much privacy and comfort for her. Also, having access to the shower was important to her when she lived in her apartment. We were able to replicate similar living accommodations. When she became weaker, it was easier to give her bed baths having the bathroom close by. Mom enjoyed warm water and if the water was too cold, I was able to change it as frequently as she liked.

Close to her death when I was giving her sponge baths, she enjoyed having her feet massaged. She had a favorite lotion that I used to massage her feet and legs that left a unique, pleasant smell. After she was gone, once I used this cream on my hands and broke into tears because the essence of this cream reminded me of her and how much she enjoyed this smell. The smell made me feel close to her again.

Shortly after she moved into our house, we realized that having her bedroom on the second floor could limit the time we spent with her during the day. When she moved in with us, she was able to walk slowly and with assistance she could go up and down the stairs. It was important for me to preserve her strength, have her feel part of the family and not make her feel limited and bed bound. Walking downstairs not only encouraged her to stay physically active but also provided a change of environment.

When she was downstairs during the day with us, she was not engaging in anything but simply observing our daily activities. She was part of the family. Sometimes she would stare blankly through the window not saying anything. Frequently her eyes rested on the garden covered with the snow. When I asked her what she was thinking, she had nothing to say.

My memories brought me back to my young years when I lived in Poland and times when Mom worked with such pleasure in the garden. She loved to plant a variety of vegetables and flowers seeds then watch how they grew. During harvesting season she would share with the neighbors the vegetables, flowers and fruits. She was very proud of her garden.

Thinking about the garden reminded me how strong she was not that long ago; and, how much effort and interest sparked in her eyes when she was engaging in any kind of garden work. At the time when she loved the garden, I absolutely despised any work related to yard work. During the warm weather one of my chores, as the oldest child, was to weed and help out with the garden and yard work. As a teenager, I was more interested in spending time with my friends rather than working with the shovel and dirt.

Fortunately, my husband shared my mother's interest in garden work. During the warm weather when my husband was working on his garden, my mother visited us. She automatically started helping with whatever he was doing in the garden. Her enthusiasm and pleasure that I remember from my young years hadn't changed. She was still as passionate about working in the garden as when I was a teenager. She told me frequently that working and observing a garden and its changes reminded her of the natural life process and how much we all change throughout life. Now I can understand why her attention was so often with the garden.

During the day when my mom was downstairs, I hoped to divert her depressed thoughts and stimulate at least a little positive thinking. To sleep and be free from pain were the only two things she desired. It was a challenge to find activities that could cheer her spirit. When she was younger and healthy, in the morning after opening the curtains she looked at the sun, said her daily prayer then usually enjoyed reading the newspapers. When she stayed with us, as soon as daylight entered the room she complained that the light aggravated her eyes and she preferred darkness. Polish newspapers, magazines or books did not create any interest.

Since she enjoyed praying I thought that listening to audiotapes of religious songs and talk might stimulate some interest. As soon as I started playing these tapes, she starting singing to herself and repeating the words of the songs. When I listened to some of these songs the melody of the music sounded so discouraging to me, but it created the opposite effect on my mom. I was so pleased that this activity captured her interest for a numbers of hours and redirected her mind at least momentarily from her sickness.

One warmer winter day in January, my mom asked to go outside to get some fresh air. I was so excited! Here was something that she wanted to do. Bundled up in a warm jacket, she sat down on the backyard bench and started deeply inhaling the cold brisk winter air. She held the air deeply inside of her lungs and with such pleasure, then slowly exhaled. I was surprised that she didn't look around in any direction. Instead her eyes were focused on the tops of the trees. As she was taking more deep breaths her face started to change color from pale to bright pink. I noted how much healthier she looked with the bright color on her face. It brought back memories of my young days in Poland when she was watching my brother and me. While we were playing she was standing and just watching our activities. Her cheeks quickly turned bright pink-red from the cold winter air. In my younger days mom was content in watching us play. Now we took opposite places. I observed with contentment how pleasurable this simple activity was to my mom.

After this brisk outside air, I thought she might enjoy a large lunch. But her appetite was poor. She was loosing weight daily since she had lost completely the interest in food.

To increase her interest in food, I thought I would prepare some of the meals she cooked for us when we were kids. Sometimes she told me what she would like to eat. As soon as I prepared the meal, she would look at the plate and not eat. I was devastated. Whatever I tried to prepare, nothing was appealing to her. I called my friend and asked her to visit and taste mom's favorite pancakes to tell me what was wrong with them. Mom was telling me the pancakes had a bad odor, were bitter and undercooked. I started to think it was my cooking that was turning Mom away from eating. My friend reassured me there was nothing wrong with my cooking. Mom's taste was completely changing. She also added I needed to accept things as they were.

I thought about the times when I was young and living with my parents. How often I had complained and criticized my mom's cooking. The only difference was that I was healthy and my complaints were unreasonable; now she was sick and her complaints had to be excused. My heart was broken from the complaints she made about my cooking. I can only imagine how discouraging it was for her to put so much effort into cooking only to hear so many complaints from my brother and me.

After numerous trials with different foods and drinks, I discovered one drink that she seemed to enjoy - Vanilla Ensure drink mixed with instant coffee and ice. I was pleased I could finally satisfy her appetite with something. I began to accept that it was not her complaining about my cooking but her disease and dying that was speaking.

Throughout years of my mom's sickness she continually amazed me with her high tolerance for pain. Even the doctors were sharing with me that she had such a stoic attitude towards pain. She did not complain until the pain was unmanageable. She expressed to me frequently that she was afraid to "be addicted" to pain medications and "God is testing my tolerance and would not give me more than I can handle." I was frequently reminding her that it was not healthy for her to be in lows and highs in pain because it takes much longer for the medications to work when these wide fluctuations occur. It really didn't matter what I said, she still believed that her pain was for a reason and she needed to handle it as it came.

In the last month of her life, Mom was experiencing excruciating pain. The doctors advised me that she would benefit from a continuous administration of morphine. She was so upset that her pain medication patches were no longer sufficient to control the pain. After one night of such severe pain, crying, and being awake all night, she agreed to a continuous morphine IV.

Here came another dilemma for me. I was responsible to adjust her drip rate based on the level of her pain. Each time when I called the hospice nurses and asked them for advice, my heart broke when I had to increase the rate of morphine. I kept thinking about the safe parameters I learned in nursing school. Slowly the dosage increased from 25 mg and finally reached 75 mg/hour. I was deeply torn inside as to how much pain she was having and how much morphine she could tolerate. The hospice nurses reassured me that it was right and okay to keep her pain level under control. I was the only one who could assess her pain level and change the dosage. As a result Mom did not need to suffer and wait for the hospice nurses to make these adjustments.

In the last month of my mother's life, hospice nurses played an important role in my mother's life and mine. No one else was able to provide the support, quick feedback and compassion as effectively as they did.

The hospice nurses also helped me to maintain the quality of Mom's life while managing her pain level. They gently made me aware that I was the one who needed to give her permission to die because I was so close to her during her illness. Mom relied very much on my word and the strength that I was giving to her. I thought that it was not true. In my heart I felt that she knew when it was her time to go and nobody would be able to stop her.

These thoughts rolled in my mind for two weeks. The hospice nurses kept reminding me that she was waiting for my permission to let go. I kept telling them that it was not the right time because my father needed to see her before she died. I felt I had no control over her death. My fears were escalating because I knew I had to face death and in my own house. How much closer could it get? I was not ready for that experience. I kept telling myself it would be much easier if she were in the hospital or where someone else could handle the situation better than me. I was hiding my fears by telling everybody that my father's arrival was important to her and that she was waiting for his permission to die, not mine.

My father arrived and was able to spend two days with my mother. He also was in a state of denial about my mother's state of health. At that moment I realized that the hospice nurses were right. Giving her my permission to die could relieve her pain and suffering. This realization made me stronger and ready to face my first death, the death of my mother. I wanted to be present at that moment without running away, hiding, or denying that death was as scary, as I had thought and exaggerated in my mind.

That last day as I got dressed for work, I felt that before leaving I wanted to talk to my mother and tell her the truth - her battle with cancer would prolong her suffering and it was time to give up her fight. As I spoke with her I gently reminded her that we had tried all the possible treatments that were available. I told her that it was time for her to be free of pain, morphine drips and other measures. I told her she could go where there would be peace and life without pain. My father sat next to me looking at me very strangely. He believed neither my words nor what I was saying.

I was able to leave her room and walked slowly downstairs. As I reached the bottom of the stairs, my father called to me. My mother had taken her last breath. As first I was mad that I wasn't there. Then I realized the hospice nurses were right. Mom had waited for my permission and she did not want to give me any more pain. So, after I left she was free to go.

I feel fortunate that I was able to spend those last six months with my mom. I was surprised how things naturally changed around. I was forced to confront many areas of my life that I never paid attention to before. I thought a lot about how I had handled things when I was young with my mother guiding me. At that time I was not paying any attention to her wisdom. Once again my mother's wisdom was coming through. My mother's fight with cancer inspired me to be a strong, independent person and face my fears.

Mom sent me a powerful final gift of wisdom that I should not be afraid of death; simply accept it when it comes. From that moment, I have never been afraid of facing anyone's death. I now know that when I am faced with one of my patient dying, I will be able to support them and not be afraid. I feel that my support for the patient and their family will be real and free of fear. I know that my fears about death are in the past because I have faced them with my mother's help. My fears of death were released in my own home by giving my mother permission to die after her long battle with colon cancer.

THIRTEEN

Intensive Caring

Gretchen Reising Cornell

When hearing of my mother's death the usual statement to me was and still is even after five years, "I'm sorry." In our culture that's what we expect, for someone to be sorry for us or the deceased. How can I say that I'm not sorry and that Mother's death was a healing experience for us both? That her death was a "good" experience? I learned a lot about myself and about her through the experience. I want nurses and everyone to know our story so that they can better help families at this time of their lives.

There is a history to our relationship that led up to my mother's death in 1997. As an only child I was expected to be a "little adult." I spent a lot of time with Mother because my father was a traveling salesman and frequently away from home. Even when he was home, however, his alcoholism made me feel that he was far away from who I really was, and what I needed. Because of frequent conflicts between my parents and me, I became a harmonizer and tried to be a "fixer" as much as my parents would let me.

Going into adulthood, my parents and I carried a lot of baggage we never were able or willing to discuss. In some way it seemed we had let each other down. Maybe if I'd been a boy instead of a girl, Dad would have liked me better. Maybe if I'd been an artist or a physician, Mother would have liked me better. Maybe if my mother didn't have polio as a child, or she had divorced my dad, or was more available to me when I needed her, or had stood up for me, or hadn't been so judgmental, or, or, or… So many "maybes" we never admitted or talked about.

After Father died I became more aware of all of the unmet needs my mother had. By then, my late husband, Pete and I had joined the Church of Jesus Christ of Latter Day Saints and were the parents of four children. My husband's health was declining and he was listed for a heart/lungs transplant. I never was able to tell Mother even though I tried; she expressed her belief that Pete wasn't "so sick," and "his doctors are just out for a lot of money," or "he just wants attention," or "MY doctor says what he has won't kill him."

Underlying her lack of understanding of my situation was her need for me to reverse our roles and take care of her. I think it was a cry for help to which I was unable to respond. Four children, a disabled husband, and living seven hours away made giving care to my mother almost impossible. I did what she would allow me to do long distance, on the phone, and by visits three to four times a year. It became increasingly evident though that her health was deteriorating. I finally insisted she schedule appointments with her physicians so I could go with her to learn what was really going on. She resisted, I think, because she did not want me to know how really ill she was and didn't want to know herself either. All ailments in her life as a young and then older adult were blamed on "when I had polio." Even obvious conditions such as chronic cough, high blood pressure and poor circulation were attributed to the "polio" and not associated with her 65 years of smoking cigarettes.

When I was finally able to go with her to her doctors, the visits were shocking. She was legally blind because of cataracts, and was ordered by her physician not to drive until they were removed. She had such poor circulation in one leg that emergency surgery was needed to improve the blood flow. All of the major arteries in her body were blocked and collateral circulation was all that was keeping her alive. Her heart was weakened by numerous "heart attacks" that were unreported and untreated. Should I somehow have known this? Why didn't she tell me all of this?

Mother, who I felt was always trying to control me, criticized my religion, my husband, and how many children I had. Mother, who didn't want to bother me and cause me any more difficulty, hadn't told me she knew her heart was "bad" simply because "sometimes my arms hurt." She denied the seriousness of her ailments and refused surgery for her eyes or circulation because she didn't want to "bother" me. Now I understood. I had to make some decisions for her and insisted that it was "no bother."

She must have surgery to save her circulation impaired leg and her life.

Reluctantly she agreed - after she drove her car to church even though she was legally blind and should not drive. "See, I can to drive." I wonder how many times I had said that to her when I was a teenager.

Well, my 80 year old mother, Ruth, agreed reluctantly to go to the hospital for the required arterial surgery to her leg. She told none of her friends she was going. I imagine she didn't want to bother them, either. Instead of letting me push her in a wheelchair into the hospital, she insisted on painfully walking so "no one will think I'm an invalid." She stood as tall as she could and held her head high. I wonder if she knew what was ahead.

I asked her if she wanted a prayer before her surgery and she said she didn't need it. Later I regretted I didn't get all the help I could for her and for me, too. My prayers didn't seem to be enough. The old joke doesn't seem so funny now. "The surgery was a success, but the patient died." That is exactly what happened to my mother.

While I waited and waited for her to return from surgery I knew something was wrong. After thirty years in nursing I knew how to read the signs. Ruth was the only patient left in the cardiac procedure area. So, when a nurse came out of the unit to get two units of blood I knew it had to be for my mother. Then another nurse came to get a urinary catheter tray. When the physician came out to talk to me, I asked if he was taking my mother to intensive care. With an amazed look he asked how I knew. The signs were evident. The surgery had not gone smoothly. The procedure took hours longer than expected. Two units of blood and a urinary catheter tray were needed. And then I discovered the surgeon had patients waiting for him in his office. He couldn't spend any more time on my mother. He was in a hurry so he quickly mentioned, "hemorrhage, leg's OK now...needed a catheter, uncooperative...sedation." As assertive as I usually am I was not comfortable asking more questions. I wanted to see my mother and determine for myself what was going on.

Saying a quick prayer in the elevator for my mother, I arrived at the Intensive Care Unit (ICU). I didn't seem to be to welcome. The nurses repeatedly said I could be at the bedside ..."When we get her settled." With oxygen by mask and without her dentures, Mother was pale and agitated. The ICU nurse had already given her the ordered large dose of medication to decrease her confusion. The cardiologist, who evidently had not gone to his afternoon office hours, said it appeared my mother, who had never taken a drink of alcohol other than a sip of wine, was going through withdrawal.

At that point I knew the physician and I were on different agendas. This was my mother, for good or for bad, in sickness and in health, through my adolescence and her menopause. She was my mother—not his "old withdrawal patient" who had smoked her arteries to death. "LISTEN TO ME", I said, "She's not a drinker and never has been." I was afraid he had written her off already because she was old, suffered from conditions created by her own actions, namely smoking, and he saw no opportunity to "cure" her. If there can be no "cure," is there no "care" either? Wasn't this Intensive CARE or was it Intensive CURE? This was the last conversation I had with this physician. He had the weekend off and a substitute was flown in by the hospital to "cover."

At that moment I became convinced there was some deeper meaning in this scenario. I had to make some important decisions now. The parent-child roles were reversed. Mother was restrained and tethered to a blood transfusion, oxygen administration, IVs and a urinary catheter. The ICU nurses were speaking loudly to her and practically holding her down.

I was the adult and Mother was the confused and frightened frail woman with childish behavior. I would take care of her and protect her. I would be her friend, her daughter, and ultimately her nurse. As a nurse, I would advocate for her if she would let me. But, the questions were: what do we do and where do we go from here?

With oxygen and the blood transfusion, Mother's agitation decreased and her mind cleared some. I told her what had happened, what was going on and that we had to "wait and see." How many times had she told me that when she didn't want to commit herself? She calmly looked at me and replied with a dry mouth through the oxygen mask, "It's from the polio." It was at this point I decided I wasn't going to contradict her as I had earlier in my life. Today it could be "from the polio."

Later that evening I felt more confident the night nurses in the ICU were competent and would take good care of my mother so I could get some sleep. Mother was still agitated but I didn't seem to be able to help. What was going on? Was she still confused? Even with a urinary catheter, my mother tried to get out of bed to use the bathroom. Although I believe in never lying to a patient, I covered the commode with a blanket and told Mother there wasn't a bathroom close by. Once again, I was the harmonizer avoiding conflict at all costs.

Fighting against soft restraints, Mother said to me, "Don't be like them. Let me go... let me go home." And, "Don't make me get mad at you!" as she slapped my hand. Instantly I was three years old again - I'd heard that before. Don't make me get mad at you. So, with our roles reversed through necessity, I told my mother as I had told so many other daughters' agitated elderly mothers, "We're going to help you...we're going to take care of you."

The next morning the fog in Mother's mind had lifted. Maybe it was from the medications, the blood transfusions, or the oxygen. Ruth, my mother as I wanted her to be, was better than ever. Although she had developed a heart arrhythmia - atrial fibrillation - her mind was clearer. I bathed her and helped to a bedside chair. We talked about her health and newly pink leg that no longer hurt. I fixed her hair and painted her fingernails. I put on her makeup. We talked about the past and the present.

She didn't want to talk about the future and said, "We'll have to see," her usual comment when she didn't want to answer, or commit, or think about something. For her saying "We'll have to see" would make all problems go away. The ICU nurses asked her as I had many times before to complete advance directives and a durable power of attorney for health care. Instead of the expected "We'll have to see," the reply was "Gretchen will know what to do."

I continuously felt I was "in the way" in the ICU. The nurses insisted that I follow their routine and respect the five minutes every hour visiting schedule. Trying this I was apprehensive and my mother became more agitated when I wasn't with her.

The day I spent with my mother in ICU was a great day though! Ruth and I were adults without the troubles and conflicts of the past. We laughed, reminisced and joked. We talked about important things and hugged a lot. The change in Ruth was dramatic. She was not only back to her usual self but a new and improved Mother. At that point I wondered, was it an answer to my prayers, or a response to the improved circulation in her leg, or something else. The change from my often crabby mother to the delirious combative patient and then to a new, improved, not seen for a long time mother was so intense I wondered if there was a deeper meaning that I didn't see? Was it a miracle in answer to prayer and would she stay that way? Or, was this the "calm before the storm" as I had seen as a nurse with dying patients… a brief time of clearness before the rapid decline.

For whatever reason that was the best day we ever had together as adults. There were no games, no hidden agendas, no secrets, no conflict, no unfinished business. Ruth and I told each other things you hope you can say before someone dies. We said we were sorry and we loved each other.

As I feared, the new, improved Ruth did not last. Her condition deteriorated that night as she started to experience increasing heart failure. The irregular heartbeat was not responding to treatment and was decreasing the amount of blood circulating throughout her body. She was going into kidney failure. We had been given the gift of a day to repair our relationship, strengthen the foundation of our eternal relationship, and say goodbye. I wished my children could have seen her that day.

I told Ruth her kidneys and heart were failing and I had declined putting her on a ventilator to prolong her dying. She shook her head as if saying, "Yes" and through the oxygen mask I thought she mouthed, "It's the polio."

When it became evident that Mother would not live through the night, the ICU nurses insisted that I would be more comfortable in a private room with my mother. I preferred to stay in the ICU because of the monitoring so I could know exactly her physiological status plus I didn't want to disturb my mother with a move at that point in time. She only had a few hours to live. I feel the nurses would have been more comfortable with us in a private room where they didn't have to see me, alone, with my dying mother.

Surprisingly, I was not devastated knowing my mother was dying. We had been given two amazing experiences to prepare us both for her death. I had been allowed to see and experience what her quality of life probably would have been like if Ruth had lived - debilitated, delirious, unhappy, sedated and unable to care for herself. The second event was a beautiful day of joy, companionship and enjoyment in each other's company. I had the opportunity to really express my love for Mother and to give her a little piece of the care she had given to me so many times in my life.

I believe that was God's preview for us of heaven. Ruth would suffer if she lived and thus was allowed by God to leave this earth. Not only was I able to see and experience what it would be like for Ruth to stay on earth but also to experience what it would be like for her in heaven. She could be happy and cheerful.

With courage and peace Ruth did not fight the inevitable. Shortly before her heart stopped Ruth reached her arms upward to an unseen Presence. She was unable to tell me if she saw or felt someone there. I laid on her bed with her and sang "I Am a Child of God" over and over until her heart slowed and stopped. The ICU nurses cried with me and felt someone should be called so I wouldn't be "alone."

I didn't feel alone. My connection to my mother and maybe to God was the deepest I had ever had. The connection was beyond words and a transcendent "oneness." It was a peace, which passes understanding.... a great stillness of peace, joy and freedom. I knew my mother felt it too…. a felt knowing and being with God.

I don't sing very well but I know the love and the Spirit that were with us touched the nurses. The ICU nurses who came to be with us shared their feelings of calmness and connection. I believe the hand of God was on us and blessing everyone around with the sacredness of this moment. It wasn't just another old lady dying, it was someone's mother changing from mortal to immortal. It was a privilege to be present - not a duty.

So, this is the story of Ruth's death. I'm not sorry she died because otherwise we would not have had our special day together. I had the opportunity to be with her when she died. Ruth did not cause a car accident or suffer a serious fall as often occurs in older adults. She lived independently and in her own way. Her passing was a beginning not an ending for both or us.

How has this experience changed me and given me wisdom? Well, I've written this account of the experience and shared the sacredness of her passing. Her death was not the transforming moment for us—it was the day that we had together. That was the day when we experienced what eternity could be… love - pure love. My mother gave me a spiritual second birth. I am now a better nurse, a better mother, a better teacher; and, I now live with an eternal perspective. I now am not shy about kissing the dying patient goodbye or praying for a smooth passing. I thank God and my mother for who I am and am becoming.

Postscript

What if I had missed this opportunity to be with my mother when she died? What if I had not been "allowed" to be with her in the ICU? Did I have to be given permission by staff and policies to care for my mother and be truly present with her? It is a privilege to be with a dying person and experience her passing. What if I had missed it and gone to the hotel when the night nurse told me to "get some rest?" Nurses have the responsibility to provide families with the opportunity to experience what my mother and I had together. Nurses often can make things happen for families rather than not just waiting for things to happen. Because I advocated for my mother and myself, we had the experience of *Intensive Caring* and the healing of our relationship.

FOURTEEN

A Legacy of Love

Mary A. Helming

On November 5, 2003, my wonderful mother, Florence M. Blaszko, transitioned from this life to the next. Although she had suffered from endless pain over many preceding years, her passing came as a shock to all who knew her. A soft, warm-hearted woman, my mother was a friend to all. She was gifted as a cook, and her friends and family all benefited from her delicious foods. Without regard to herself, she always sought first to care for my brother, my father and me. In my early years, I recall times when she went without new clothing or items she desired, in order that she might better provide for us. She would often tell me that she needed little in life, as long as she had the love and companionship of her husband. Truly, my dear mother taught me that the essential things in life couldn't be bought with money; they are family and friends.

Worn down after many years of suffering from unrelenting back pain and sciatica, crippled with arthritis, spinal stenosis, and osteoporosis, at age 84, she sometimes told my father she didn't know if she could handle the pain any longer. Coupled with serious cardiovascular disease and congestive heart failure, her activities became increasingly limited and she became, to some extent, housebound.

I longed to bring her places and to shop with her as we used to in days of old. Yet no longer could she tolerate even lengthy car rides, which would exacerbate her pain. Despite all of these ills, she remained cheerful and loving to the end. There was always a smile on her face and always she waited eagerly for her children's and grandchildren's phone calls and visits. Mom was far more interested in hearing about everyone else's lives than in complaining about her own. Her bravery amazes me still.

In October 2003, my Mom happily accompanied her husband and family to a joyful celebration: my father's 85th birthday. Just a week before, my mother had been by my side waiting for my father to come through cataract surgery. I watched as she lovingly tended to this man, the man who had been the foundation of her life. How proud she was of him. It was as though she had accompanied him through these final events and now she could go to her rest. Strangely enough, two events happened just one month before the October birthday and surgery. Two old family friends precipitously came to visit my Mom. She had not seen either of these people for many years. I recall her telling me that she wondered if that meant she was going to die soon, and I, of course, dismissed that very notion.

However, suddenly, on November 1, she fell down her cellar stairs, stairs which she had been avoiding as we told her not to go on them due to her unsteady gait. We do not know what happened to her; perhaps she fainted, perhaps she suffered a cardiac event, or perhaps her internal defibrillator fired and propelled her downstairs. She was found, severely injured but still conscious, at the bottom of the stairs by my grieving father. Because of being on an anti-coagulant medication, her bleeding was more severe. She suffered intracerebral hemorrhages and multiple facial and extremity fractures.

I was watching my son's final award-winning marching band competition when I finally turned on my cell phone and received the phone message. I will never forget that call from my father. Paralyzed with fear, I called one hospital. She was no longer there, but had been transferred to another trauma center with neurosurgical coverage. I tried desperately to obtain information about it, only to be halted by the new HIPPA regulations that prohibited medical and nursing staff from talking to me over the phone. I was without transportation; I had journeyed over an hour's drive to this band competition by school bus, accompanying the band as a chaperone. Finally, some dear family friends who had driven themselves to the venue saw my plight, and agreed to leave early to bring me to the hospital my mother was now in.

Frantically, I prayed without ceasing on that longest journey of journeys to the hospital. Alone, I entered the emergency room. As a nurse, I thought I knew what to expect. As a daughter, seeing my mother bruised, sutured, and in severe pain was more than I could bear. I asked her what happened and she moaned that she did not want to talk about it. Then, I told her I loved her, and she said "I know." Those were to be her last words to me. I was the only member of the family who got to speak with her before she worsened and intubated - a tube put into her lungs to breathe. She said her last words to me. What a painful privilege that was.

I watched fearfully as her blood pressure dropped and she began the descent into shock. Bags of fluid and blood were transfused. At last she was moved to the Intensive Care Unit. Finally, members of my family began to appear. There we were precipitously forced to make the decision to have her intubated. Questions, questions, questions were hurled upon us. Was there a living will? Did we want her fully resuscitated? Did we want her resuscitated only under certain conditions? We were not prepared. I doubt any family members are ever really prepared, no matter how much they think they are.

Five days passed. We stood vigil as it was determined my Mom had suffered her third heart attack, and her organ systems began the precipitous process of failure-the heart, the lungs, the liver, and the kidneys. The ICU protocol called for sedating patients so we only were given brief moments to try to converse with Mom while she struggled to open her eyes. Her sad, weary eyes told us she loved us but were filled with anguish and fear. With heart wrenching difficulty, I stayed with her in the room, speaking to her even though she lay asleep and sedated, with impaired consciousness. I had always heard people in comas could still likely hear. By day four, her eyes were glazed and she stared blankly ahead. That which I feared, the comatose state from her collected traumas, had come to pass. Her eyes did not open again, even when the sedating intravenous medication was halted momentarily. What were we to do?

She had signed a living will. We knew she did not want to suffer. Yet still, it was ever so painful to make the decision we knew was facing us. My father could not say it was time for her to go. My brother struggled endlessly with the decision, hoping to bide time until his children in college could finish their exams to come say goodbye. My teenage son stoically came to say goodbye. How he had loved his grandma. It pained me so to watch his pain. My sister-in-law, a former intensive care nurse, was an angel to me, staying overnight with me that first endless night in the hospital and walking us all through what was happening with Mom. I became the primary contact person, dealing with the nurse practitioners, nurses, and physician's assistants who cared for Mom daily. Rarely, did we see a physician in person. Instead, we had to rely upon telephone calls from a physician to substitute for the comfort of speaking with someone live.

Mom's pacemaker/automated internal defibrillator was failing to halt her increasingly erratic heart rhythms. My sister-in-law and I recognized Mom would likely go into cardiac arrest because of the increasing number of premature heart contractions she was suffering that were moving into runs of ventricular tachycardia – rapid heart beats. The internal defibrillator had served its time; it no longer could manage her dying heart.

Strangely, I found an electrocardiogram rhythm strip on Mom's bedside table. A run of ventricular tachycardia was prominent. This was the signal to us that Mom might die when we weren't there to hold her and comfort her.

The family finally made a decision that we desired to be with her when she transitioned to the next life. At last, that fateful decision had to be made. On the fifth day, in early evening, my father, my brother, my sister-in-law, my husband, and I made a unified decision. It was time to let Mom go. She had suffered too much. We could not watch her deteriorate any further. Her pain was too severe; our pain was too severe.

Quickly, the staff set things in motion. The hospital chaplain and minister were called in. The wonderful nurse who supported us through this, made the room tranquil by dimming the lights and drawing the curtains. We all pulled chairs around the bed and surrounded Mom in a circle. Prayers were said by the chaplain and minister. Comforting words were expressed to us all. Then we were left alone with Mom. We read from the Bible the 23rd Psalm, to comfort us and we hoped, to comfort Mom. We prayed the Lord's Prayer all together, grasping each other's hands and holding onto Mom as she lay in her bed. The room took on an air of tranquility. It was ethereal. There is no other way to describe the moment.

The nurse came to make Mom comfortable with a final dose of morphine before she was removed from the respirator. How foreign she looked - not at all like herself. She had been so beautiful, even to her 84th year. Now she was bruised in her face and her beautiful hair, permed just the week before she fell ill, was flattened. This was not my Mom. No, my Mom was going away to a better place…a place of peace where she would suffer no more. It took only minutes for her to transition. We watched her blood pressure and pulse slowly drop and we heard her last breath. We held on to each other in our circle as we held on, each of us, to part of Mom's body, helping her in the only way we knew how. We told her unceasingly how much we loved her. My Dad gave her a final kiss. Then we all kissed her. My husband said "Now she is an angel." It was hard to believe. No, it can't be this fast. Yet there was an unearthly sense of peace hovering in the room, and I believe I felt Mom slip away into the great white light that we hear so much about. How difficult it must have been for her to leave us all. She loved her family more than anything else.

The kind nurse lovingly gave us clay handprints of Mom and locks of her hair. Each grandchild, each child, and my father received this last gift. I did not want to go. I did not want to leave Mom. Yet we had to go. She would have wanted us to go on. I promised her I would take care of Dad. He has lived with us part of the time since, and I hope Mom looks down on us, happy that we have helped Dad to manage. She loved him so. He loved her so. I loved her so.

Our family came together to plan her service. It was a beautiful service, as many had said. We chose beautiful cards for remembrance, cards that said "Don't grieve for me, for now I'm free." My 18 year-old son did a reading and was a pallbearer. I was so proud of him, and I know his Grandma was so proud of him, as well. A nephew gave another reading. My husband gave a eulogy, as did I. We focused on the wonderful things she did in her life. We celebrated her life and despite our grief, celebrated that she was free of pain, free of her years of suffering. We found the list of hymns she wanted sung and we sang as the organ played. My brother-in-law sang a beautiful solo in her honor. It was indeed a celebration of a beautiful woman and her wonderful life.

As we journeyed to the cemetery, I heard my Mom's voice, comforting me. It was so real. I still hear her voice at times, and I truly do believe she can talk with me and I with her. Leaving her at the cemetery, on a harsh, windy and bleak November day, was one of the hardest things I have ever done. I remembered so vividly a poem I had asked my Dad to read at my wedding just five years before. Thank goodness Mom got to see me remarried and happy again. Thank God for that. This marriage poem, heard on a Christian radio station, ended with the story of one spouse placing the other in the arms of God at the end of life. I remember how my Dad fought to keep back tears as he read this at my wedding. Now, I fight to keep back tears as I remember how we all placed her in the arms of God, the loving, strong, ever-forgiving arms of God.

Today, as I write this, floods of memories pour over me. It has been nearly two years since Mom has left us. I still see her beautiful smiling face and twinkling eyes looking lovingly at me every time I walk into her home and see her empty chair. Her house is almost exactly as she left it. Her clothes are almost exactly as she left them. We want it that way. It comforts us immeasurably.

What I miss most about Mom is being able to talk to her. How we loved talking together on the phone or in person. I could say anything to Mom, and she would always show caring and love. She loved to hear about our lives, to know everyone was alright. She was unhappy if any of us were unhappy. Indeed, she lived for us. Sometimes, I forget she is gone and when I am especially sad or especially happy, or if I have news to tell, I think to myself "I need to call Mom." Then, I have to remind myself there is no phone to reach her. So silently, I talk to her and tell her about my life. I have asked for her guidance when I did not know which way to turn. I believe she guided me. I hear her words to me still, words of concern, of love. These words do not die; they have an eternal life in my heart and my mind.

Since Mom has gone, I have moved ever closer to my spiritual side. I want to know God and to speak to Him daily. I believe my Mom must be very happy to be with her loved ones, especially her own Mom, whom she lost in her tender teen years. I count myself blessed to have had my Mom with me for all my life until she died. Many daughters are not so fortunate.

It is especially now that I think of Mom because three weeks ago, I became the legal guardian of an eleven year-old girl whose own Mom is at this moment lies dying in Hospice of aggressive cancer at the age of 54. There was no family for this little girl, as she was adopted. Writing this essay makes me remember how very difficult it was to lose my Mom at the age of 84. It is hard to conceive how difficult it will be for this little girl to lose her Mom at the age of 54, when she has barely reached her adolescent years.

Will I ever be able to replace my little girl's mother? No, never. A mom is unique and she, too, will live on in the memory of my little girl. Maybe, in some small way, I can understand the pain of this eleven year-old, because the pain of my Mom's passing is still as fresh today as it was two years ago. Perhaps, I will honor the memory of her Mom and of my Mom, by passing on to her the traditions my Mom set in motion. Shopping excursions, ladies' lunch out, cooking together, helping with childcare, giving advice, and mostly, being there to listen, are all ways I can honor my Mom as I take over in this new role as legal guardian. I feel the presence of my mother watching over me, telling me that everything will be all right, even though we must pass through some unsettled and uncharted waters right now. I will learn as much as I can about my little girl's mother, to pass on the knowledge of how wonderful a human being she was. This is the best gift I can give my little girl.

I am sure Mom is very happy for me. She knew I always wanted a daughter, too. My Mom will be looking over my shoulder, watching me. The memories of how she raised me as a daughter will strengthen and guide me.

Because of Mom, I am led to read increasingly more about life after death experiences, about opening my spirit to listen to the voice of the Absolute, the Sacred Source.

Mom was an incredibly good person. She is someone I aspire to be though I fall through incessantly. She was an oasis of peace in my life, and her image of quiet acceptance is one I seek to emulate. I could feel calmness around her, and increasingly, it is calmness and peace that I seek. In my often frenetic, harried life, I long for the peace and calmness that surrounded Mom. Her example is like a beacon in my life that I aspire to reach.

Her life was all about her family and this is a legacy she has passed along to me. No matter what else I accomplish in my work and career, my family will always be my most important treasure. Being a mother is the most important role I will ever play in this life. I can say this because I had the best of mothers; and, she taught me about what was truly important in life. In her quiet ways, she honored God and in so doing, has taught me to honor God and live honorably.

My Mother left a legacy of love, which is unceasing. Her love will become the love I pass on to my children. I love you, Mom. Thank you for being there for me all of your life. Thank you for giving me life, for giving me hope, and for giving of yourself. I could not have asked for a better mother.

FIFTEEN

The Contract

Sophia Swaner

My mother and I made a contract long before I came into this body. She agreed to bring me into the world and I agreed to help her leave it. Looking back, it seems a fair and equitable exchange of love and support one for another. You might say I had the more difficult task, but mother was the strong one, the courageous one. What she gave to me was the greatest gift, the greatest blessing a mother could ever give her daughter.

Growing up with mom and dad was always fun. I loved to watch them dance in the dining room as they played the 45 rpm records on the phonograph. Often friends came over for parties and get togethers and our family came to visit us a lot.

My mother loved pretty clothes and liked to dress up. My sister and I always had matching outfits and accessories and our haircuts, well, they made us look like twins. I remember going to costume parties and the fun mom would have dressing us all up in our costumes and then going together as a family. Through my childhood eyes, everything seemed so perfect, lovely and exciting. It was only when we moved to a new town after my Dad took a new job that things began to change.

It was the loss of my Mother to my Dad's best friend that brought me to be raised by my Dad and his parents. At eight years old, I suddenly found myself living with my paternal grandparents and deeply missing my Mother. The only explanation that I was given was that Mother had once again been hospitalized for her nerves. They didn't know when she would be coming home. Well I remember the day my Mother took such time and care ironing our little dresses and packing our clothes. I was told that we, my younger sister and I, were being sent off to grandmother's for a short visit. Thinking back, I now understand why my tender feelings and emotions fought with such resistance to just stay home that day. In the deepest part of my soul, I knew that it would be a long time before I returned home to live again with my Mom. In a twist of fate some forty years later, my Mom came home to live with me. For the first time since that painfully agonizing day, Mother and I were finally living under the same roof together. At last, great joy and peace flooded my soul.

There were times in those early years, after my parent's separation, when all I wanted was to be with my Mother. I really didn't want to live with my dad and grandparents. But, I was told to tell the judge that I wanted to live with my Dad. Well, of course I did just that. My father had a way of making his will known and feared by all. I looked forward to the one weekend a month when my Mom would drive down from Nashville. Picking up the two of us we would spend the weekend with her and her new husband, my Dad's ex-best friend.

I lived with my Dad until I graduated from high school. My sister left home in the tenth grade when I left for college. She moved in with Mother. I always felt great love and support from my Mother even though we lived miles apart. She was always there at birthdays, Christmas and one weekend a month. My Mother exposed me to many cultural experiences. I had opportunities to go to museums, movies, vacations and unique places thanks to my mother's insistence. I fully embrace all of the experiences of my life with her. I was a very blessed young girl. As such I honor her in death as I did in life.

One Wednesday afternoon in May about two years prior to Mother's passing, the phone rang at my business and my half brother's broken voice told of the passing of his Dad unexpectedly from a heart attack. My stepfather had taken care of my Mother for the past fifteen years almost hand and foot. What was she going to do now without him? Her failing health, pain and discomfort made it difficult for her to be less than dependent on her husband. Mom had not prepared for the possibility that he would pass before her. My mind raced as I longed to get to my Mother and comfort her. All I could think of was how to help her get through this. I was soon to see that my Mother was made of pure strength and courage with a mind of steel in a frail, weak body.

We arranged for Mother to live at home and have a caregiver during the daytime. My uncle's company installed a security system with a med alert feature and my two siblings and I felt mom would be safe. Later on we moved her to an assisted living facility. Unhappy there, she decided to sell her house and move in with me. I was the only child who could take her. I welcomed the opportunity with open arms and heart.

Over the years Mother had been a surgical nurse and ended her nursing career under the direct auspices of a well-known ear nose and throat specialist. Mom loved her work and gave countless hours of dedicated service to her nursing. A perfectionist, nothing was left unattended. She gave whatever effort and time was required to do her job well. She was amazingly conscious of all things connected to the body. On mention of any symptom, you could count on a sequence of questions to follow leading to a diagnosis. More often than not she was right on the money and we knew what to do right away. She totally believed in her profession and the Gods and Goddesses of the white coats who reigned. Mother always did as her doctors told her to do. In her last few years she took twenty-four meditations a day. Her routine was so well grounded that no force could change it in any way. She was always planning ahead and getting prepared for the next day. Merrily singing she enjoyed her television programs as she busily moved through each day.

The first year we spent together was rocky. Mom was very needy and didn't like being alone. I, on the other hand, was self-sufficient and cherished my alone time. It took us about eight months to get used to each other and this new family constellation. I was consistently amazed at her determination to keep going. Determined to make the very best of a failing body, her spirit and her love for her children and grandchildren gave her the ambition to carry on. Even though she became more cautious with activity and relied more on ambulatory devices to support her, her fun loving and caring spirit were very apparent. We enjoyed many wonderful days together. Watching movies, enjoying nice dinners and outings to the mall to shop for pretty clothes were highlights of our last years together.

Since having asthma as a young child, Mother was quite often hospitalized with pneumonia over the years. The fact that she was a smoker for twenty-five years certainly didn't help. During our time living together we had several emergency room visits and numerous hospitalizations. It seemed that no matter how sick she became her spirit to live always won out. After approximately ten surgeries and a lifetime of hospitalizations, my mother wasn't giving up on her life. She loved life and she wanted to live it to the fullest for as long as she could. There were many times that we became restless with her constant trips to the doctors and her never-ending complaints of this and that. Nonetheless, she would bounce back and be asking to go out for dinner and go shopping.

I learned to set boundaries with my Mother, sort of like parents do when they are raising children. The boundaries seemed a necessary step for maintaining my family's mental health. During that time my eldest son and husband retreated to the den and spent most of their time there.

I worked each day and in the evenings always planned a nice dinner with Mother, either prepared at home or takeout. She loved meat and three vegetables with cornbread. So often I would stop at the local diner on my way home and get carryout. We would sit at the glass top dining room table and enjoy our food together and talk about our day and laugh a lot. Of course, she might be in a complaining mood, so I just had to take whatever came and sometimes it wasn't all bliss.

She amazed me with her change of emotions during a conversation. One minute she was complaining and the next we were talking about what she would do tomorrow. Shopping sprees were planned and helping her select outfits to try on became my job. It was difficult getting her ambulatory devices through the isles so I seated her in the dressing room and would run her outfits to try on and make a day of it. Mother had excellent taste and was very meticulous, a perfectionist actually. All clothes must fit just so and have properly matching accessories. During the later months of her life, she never gave up her love for shopping, going out to eat and spending time with her family. I guess that is what kept her going especially after the death of her beloved husband. She told me more than once that we were all she had to live for and she lived it well.

One Sunday afternoon we were sitting at the kitchen table enjoying lunch together. I clearly saw the agony and pain she was having as she struggled to sit and make the very best of things. I felt her pain and her struggles, actually felt them inside of me. I heard myself asking her, "Mother why do you keep fighting so hard? I know it hurts you so badly to move and to just sustain every day's existence. Why not just let the things take their natural way?" She looked deep into my eyes then slowly said, "I have never been one to give up, Susan." Wow! Was that the truth! Her fighting spirit and relentless desire to press forward had often put her in the hospital when she had over taxed her body. She would rest, rejuvenate and get right back into action.

One Sunday during lunch, as we ate our coconut cake and sipped our iced tea, I suggested again that she allow nature to take its course. "Mother, you know Heaven is not a bad place to be. I think you will like it there. It will be alright if you choose to leave the pain of your body and go there, I'll understand." It felt as if my soul was talking to hers and saying it is time and I will help you. Within six weeks, my mother was making her transition with me at her side talking to her and guiding her toward the light.

It was June. We were having a hot summer with lots of rain. Mom didn't like to get out in the rain, as she feared its affects on her body. Each Sunday I tried to have a special lunch with her and share some time together. We would talk about many things. Mom was very opinionated and was confident in her position on issues. One subject we had never broached in any depth was her impending death and dying. The only reference she had ever made to me regarding her death was that she had a photo of her in her Bible that she wanted us to use for her obituary. Once she also talked briefly about what might happen if she couldn't get her breath. "I don't want to feel like I can't breathe. Please don't let me suffocate." Due to all the respiratory problems she had suffered over the years, her greatest fear was the struggle for breath.

Ultimately, respiratory issues did develop again with a return to the hospital. A failing heart and lungs, along with other major internal organs, necessitated the use of a ventilator to breathe. Gratefully, she was unconscious and didn't know what was happening. Her abstract mind, no longer focusing her awareness through her physical eyes, was becoming free. Although I didn't know at the time what was happening, I have since learned so much through study. With unconsciousness our abstract mind or soul, no longer focuses its awareness through our physical body. Our spiritual body gains strength as energy transfers to the spiritual planes of life. We actually are more "alive" than ever before. And, death (extinction into nothingness) is impossible. As a human misconception, death becomes nothing more than a fear-laden thought.

As I sat quietly at her bedside, Mom opened her eyes. I assured her it was all right to let the machine breathe for her and support her. She did not resist. There was a peace deep within her eyes I had never seen before. Her spirit was calm as she gently allowed the course of her life's journey to take her where it would. Mother no longer requested pain medication, which the doctors and nurses were much more concerned with her taking than she or I. Mother had taken pain pills for the past fifteen years to ease her body pain. In this final hour, she desired nothing to affect her mind. This was amazing to me, for in times past, she was most persistent in calling for drugs to alter her consciousness. Later I learned withholding drugs that cause unconsciousness allows the mind maximal opportunity to function with full spiritual awareness. In so doing she met God face-to-face and felt oneness with the highest planes of heaven. On some level mother must have known this.

For several days the ventilator breathed for mother as she was in and out of consciousness. I was struggling with the very real possibility that I may never be able to talk with her again or hear her voice. I wondered if there were things she wanted to say to me that hadn't been said. After three or four days, I arrived one morning to find her sitting up in bed eating peppermints with a fan blowing in her face. I walked into her room and her smile and glow from her deep blue eyes spoke to my soul. "Susan" she said, "I had a dream and I was in this beautiful place talking to God. I told God, God I love you so much, so very much, and this was the most beautiful place, so beautiful that I cannot even describe it. There is room there for all of us. Susan, I want you to promise that you will meet me there someday." I quietly replied, "I will, Mom" as I felt our deep peace and love one for another deepen even further and merge.

As I sat beside her bed there were not a lot of words exchanged. There was no need for me to say anything. I quietly, patiently waited for her to speak and say anything she needed to say.

In a childlike tone she asked me, "Why don't you crawl up here beside me and lay your little head on the pillow." Somewhat awkwardly, I released the bed rail and lowered the head of the bed. I gently snuggled up beside her and lay my head on her pillow as she spoke to me.

She softly placed her right hand on my left cheek and said, "You've been good to me, Susan. I did a terrible thing, but I just couldn't take it anymore."

Immediately I felt an overwhelming surge of gratitude for the moment. To seize this moment with total love and forgiveness was soothing to my soul. It was not just my hurtful childhood memories but the pain my mother must have felt too that was being healed. We were forgiving each other as well as ourselves for all the absences of our past.

I told her I understood and then she said, "That's an awfully lot to understand." I assured her that I did and her heart seemed at rest.

She continued, "As long as you can forgive me, I will not worry."

I reassured her that I forgave her. I understood and I loved her very much. We lay there for a long time holding each other, experiencing tremendous love one for another and deep appreciation for this time together.

For the next couple of days, I could sense Mother's consciousness going in and out of her body. I felt her soul was preparing to make its transition. I knew that natural death begins at a cosmically appointed time. According to the motives of the soul the timing is always right. My heart's desire was just to be there and support my mother to make her transition and guide her toward the light of God. I knew I could be strong for her and bring peace and love to her without consequence. I grounded my energy of unconditional love for her as I watched her breathe out and walk out of her body without pain, without fear, without resistance.

The night before mom's transition into the light, I stayed all night with her. She was in and out of consciousness and occasionally would say things. Many times that evening I heard her say "they're at the door... I've got to pull, pull... quickly, quickly." Having seen family members in her dream of heaven, I can only believe that the family was waiting for her. It appeared to take some effort for her soul to release from the body.

In the evening after coming off the ventilator, which the doctors never expected her to do, mother said, "I saw Jude on TV tonight and he looked so good". Jude, my eldest son, was living in L.A. and had not been able to fly home to see mom. Right before he left town in the spring, he had visited her in the hospital and asked if he could photograph her. He brought her buttercups in a vintage coke bottle that day. Mother dearly loved Jude and delighted in anything he did. I thought perhaps she was just thinking of him since he certainly wasn't on TV that night. In retrospect, I wonder if mom did see Jude in her dream, as some fifteen months later he would join her in the land of light. Could she have seen things I had yet to know? Does our awareness become so expanded at death that we see everything all at once?

Just before mother's ascension, I was beeped while in the coffee shop. I was told that mother was showing signs of less and less intake of life force. I returned to the Intensive Cardiac Care Unit minutes later. I said, "Mother, I am here, it is okay to go toward the light, feel the love of God and follow the love."

During the dying process I believe the Kundalini rises striking each chakra in turn and opens it to fullness. As it opens the heart chakra it may re-activate the physical body momentarily to say goodbye to loved ones. Mother opened her eyes to say goodbye and closed them peacefully as I held her hand, our cheeks touching, and whispered in her ear one last time, "I love you."

How many daughters can say, "My mom saw heaven and talked to God and asked me to join her there some day? And oh, by the way it is so beautiful beyond description and there is plenty of room there for everybody?" I have received a rare and precious gift from the passing of my mother - a firm confirmation of everlasting life and beauty where only love abounds. Heaven is real, God is there and all the family members and those friends we love too. How does it get any better than this?

This gift can never be taken from me for it lives in my heart and guides me forever. Thank you, my dear, precious mother.

SIXTEEN

Language of the Butterfly

Pam Parsons

My journey to death with my mother began simply enough. I got a phone call from her one December evening in 1997, saying she hadn't felt quite right and had a "wheeze" each time she took a deep breath. When I heard the tone of her voice, I felt a knot developing deep inside my gut.

Dad and Mom had gone to see their trusted doctor and he had discovered a spot on her right lung. Mother had been a smoker for most of her adult life, so as a nurse myself, it was no surprise to me that she had lung cancer. Although she put on a brave front, I knew that on the inside she was a scared little girl grappling with the dark unknown that any cancer diagnosis brings, and frankly, so was I.

Relationships between mothers and daughters are very unique and extremely complex. I don't pretend to have unfolded all the layers of my own, but I have searched my heart and done some gut-wrenching work to come to terms with my mother, myself, our relationship, and ultimately, her death. Realizing the cyclical nature of our mother-daughter relationship and the driving forces behind the familial patterns we seemingly perpetuated was daunting. Achieving insight and mustering the inner strength to confront these patterns and ultimately changing them is yet another step in my process of self-acceptance, self-understanding and learning as I came to terms with the death of my mother.

Mother's death remains a powerful life experience; the opportunity has been like no other. In this ultimate opening of my heart I chose to simultaneously gain the ability to harness the amazing power around the grieving process and direct it towards a deeper understanding and love of my new motherless self. And now here is the rest of my story.

From the beginning Mother opted for minimal treatment of her lung cancer-choosing palliative care (radiation only) rather than the recommended surgery. The outcome seemed inevitable to me. It was just a matter of time.

Fortunately, Mother lived well with her cancer and did not have many of the typical side effects from her treatment. She went into remission for 18 months, and then had a reoccurrence in the same lung. Her treatment options were more radiation and palliative chemo. Nina liked to call it "chemo lite." The rest of the family and I began to relax a bit. Maybe we weren't going to lose her after all.

In early 2001, about three years after her initial diagnosis, our family began to notice some mental changes in my very quick-witted, observant and articulate mother who never forgot anything.

Mother became somewhat easily flustered in a child-like way, and had difficulty expressing herself. She would repeatedly leave her purse in the Wal-Mart shopping cart, but the most noticeable change was in her once-defiant and somewhat belligerent and domineering personality and attitude. Mother became very sweet and compliant, nearly a complete opposite of how she had always been. My sister and I joked that because of her cancer, she had finally become the mother we had always wanted, and even though we tried to resist, we fell in love with her.

In December of 2001, another difficult phone call came from Mother. She had been diagnosed with metastasis to the brain. Even though I wasn't surprised, I was devastated, as was my sister. Mother again mustered up her faith, courage and stamina, and began a series of full brain radiation treatments. She continued to live her normal life with my Dad and she insisted on driving them both to and from her treatments - 25 miles one way- as she had for the past three and a half years. We held hope in our heart of hearts; she could beat her cancer…she was, after all, our invincible Nina!

Driving back and forth for six months Mother completed her treatment on June 20, 2002. As was their routine after her treatments, and on this last treatment day, they went to my sister's house for a celebratory lunch. While helping to clear the table Mother slipped on the tile floor, hitting her head very hard. An ambulance was called and she was transported to the hospital.

After several frantic long distance phone calls from my sister, I finally reached my mother in the

Emergency Room. Mother was angry as hell that she had been taken to the hospital, saying, "This is just ridiculous!" I actually felt a wave of relief come over me because this attitude and response was typical for my Mother...the one I had known all my life! She was released the next day and appeared to be OK. During the following week she began having trouble with nausea and vomiting and again she was hospitalized, this time without a fight. I felt this gnawing feeling inside my heart and gut that was too scary for me to acknowledge.

Living in another state, I decided to call Mother's oncologist and get some information. I am the kind of person who needs some "facts" to help me process. Dr. Hawkins said he thought she had "six to nine months" to live. Although this was a big shock, I decided to have a conversation with the nurse practitioner. As gently and as kindly as she could, the nurse told me that in her opinion, Mother might have "only a few weeks" to live. I cannot describe the fright and shock I felt. All I knew was it was time for me to fly home to be with her. As I boarded the plane for the long flight home, the realization hit me I could be going to help my Mother die. Feeling that inner shakiness that comes with the knowing that you are moving into an unavoidable situation with probably an unhappy ending, I spent the flight in a semi numb state.

After flying all day with my own adult daughter, Cori, by my side for support, I walked into Mother's hospital room. My tiny Mother looked pale yellow against her white hospital sheets. She had her familiar red "babushka" (this is the term she used for a bandana) tied over her baldhead. Her thin-skinned, age-marked, but still beautiful hands smoothed her sheets. "Well, Pamela", she said angrily but very weakly, "It took you long enough to get here!" then with a tone of shear helplessness she said, "Isn't this a hell of a mess?" I can only hope my face didn't convey my thoughts. What I wanted to do was sweep her up into my arms and somehow make all this horror go away. I wanted to hold her like she had held me as a little girl and make everything all better, but there was no way out. It was not going to get all better - not even close.

No one can predict when someone is going to die, but as a medical professional, there are clear signs and symptoms. In spite of the contradictions going on inside me between the "nurse" and the "daughter," I knew what I was seeing. After Mom spent a couple of days in the hospital to control her nausea, the doctors finally told our family, all gathered in the hall outside my Mother's hospital room, that on her most recent scans there was more cancer in her lungs and brain. Her doctor said that awful (yet somehow familiar) phrase no one wants to hear, "We've done everything we can and now it is time for Hospice." My heart sunk so deeply into my body, I wasn't sure it was there anymore.

Sharing the news with Mom, in spite of her mental impairment she fully understood what was happening. From her expression, I could see she went into shock. The next day when the Hospice nurse came in to talk to her about Hospice services, my Mother asked if anyone ever "got well on Hospice?" The nurse explained that indeed they did have "Hospice graduates." Mother's coping was to declare that she was going to be a "Hospice Graduate," after all, she had beaten the big C for the past four years, hadn't she? The family coped by desperately believing she could do it again. There, honestly, was a part of me that thought if anyone could beat this cancer, Mother could. This magical child-like thinking helped my slowly let all this in.

After the room had cleared, Mother asked me if I thought she was going to get better. I could see the vulnerability and trust in her eyes asking me this question. I also felt she needed what few defenses she had left, intact. So I took the emotional back door out and replied, "Well, Mother, you will either get better or you won't." "Hummm", she muttered. She had certain gestures, certain looks that only a daughter knows... you know, the ones that your mother has shown you your whole life. Mother's look conveyed volumes. Our unspoken mother-daughter dance had begun. The deafening yet silent conversation went like this, "You and I both know the reality of this situation but I need to protect you and you need to protect me." The painful truth was simply too awful for either of us to say out loud. We both knew she was dying.... and sooner rather than later.

Now, Mother had a sister twelve years her junior, Wealthia, (nick-named Wendy) who died unexpectedly of heart-related diabetic complications in 1990 when she was 59 and my mother was 71. Wealthia was the "butterfly" person in our family. She had butterfly hand towels, butterfly magnets, butterfly pins she wore on her jackets, and when we sent her a card, it would always have butterflies on it. The untimely death of my Mother's little sister left her devastated. We showered Mother with butterflies to ease her grief and allow her to keep in mind that her sweet sister, in constant physical and emotional pain the last few years of her life, was now free from her diseased body. Wendy was now flying high and free with the butterflies she always wished she could emulate. So began my mother's reign as the "butterfly person" in our family.

The day before Mother came home on Hospice, my daughter, Cori, and I spent the day rearranging the small living room of my parent's home to accommodate all of the hospice equipment Mother would need. We decided we would put up all of Mother's butterflies so she could see and enjoy them from her living room hospital bed. We were desperately trying to help make her environment as inviting and welcoming as we could. Mother had a large paper mache black-dot butterfly that we placed above the head of her bed. This specific type of butterfly, bright orange and black with white dots outlining the black wings, most definitely designated that she was the butterfly QUEEN! Decorating also gave us a way to try and find some meaning in the midst of all this seemingly meaningless ritual of helping her prepare to die.

On July 3, 2002, Mother came home from the hospital. She was weak and needed a walker to get around which was a first for her at 83 years, but she was sitting up in her chair, looking fairly perky, requesting her favorite dinner.

I lovingly prepared this meal secretly hoping - and on some level believing - that it would be the spark that started her fire back on the road into another remission. She looked so tiny sitting in front of her small plate of little bits of baked chicken, creamy mashed potatoes, and her favorite ice-cold cranberry sauce. The food sat mostly untouched. As we gathered at the dining room table, we didn't know that would be our last family meal together. I could see Mother carefully watching all of us; my Dad, my sister, my brother-in-law, my daughter, and me. She was taking it all in for one last time. My dominant thought was, "Oh God, could this really be happening?"

As soon as dinner was over, we anticipated that she would begin retching and vomiting, emptying out the small amount of food in her stomach. But she kept her dinner down. I secretly hoped that this really could be the beginning of another remission.

The next morning Mother wanted a bowl of cereal. I took this as another sign that she just might actually come out of this. Dad rushed to get it for her. Little did he know that the milk he poured over it was sour. Dad talks about how if he had only checked that milk, my mother somehow, wouldn't have started the uncontrollable vomiting that began immediately following a few bites of cereal.

My daughter had to fly home to her own budding family the next day. She hugged her beloved "Gramma" knowing it was probably going to be the last time she leaned against those large soft breasts and experienced the incredibly velvet-feeling skin of her grandmother's weak arms surround her. I am not sure how Cori did it, but she got out of there without breaking down.

The coming days were very difficult and long as the reality begin to set in. Although Mother was lucid and could hold short conversations, she was eating and drinking very little. She began losing control of her bladder and lost her ability to stand up alone. With each passing day she became weaker and weaker and each time we tried to help her move in bed, she would cry out in pain we couldn't identify or diminish.

By her fifth day at home none of us could lift my mother anymore as she became unable to assist us. Being totally bedridden for the first time in her life, the Hospice nurse suggested a catheter. I could see Mother fading rapidly with each hour that passed. My heart actually felt like it was weighted down with what felt like a lead apron - the kind the dentists use when x-rays are taken. The depth of emotional pain I began to feel, I knew was unlike anything I had ever experienced.

The dreaded truth was setting in: my Mother wasn't going to be a Hospice graduate. She was really dying and dying more quickly than we had ever anticipated. Fortunately, my sister, Patsy, Dad, and I were staying at my Mom and Dad's home so we could care for her and each other throughout this short but intense process.

Mother's pain levels began to get out of control more frequently. She moaned terribly whenever we attempted to change her bed or give her a bed bath. Hospice, the angels of mercy that they are, came with liquid morphine. Each day I would be the one to administer and carefully record the amount of morphine that was given to her to keep her comfortable.

The nurses began to gently teach us about the stages of dying and what to look for to help us monitor the rapid progression Mother was making towards her death. They gave us a book entitled, *Final Gifts,* written by two very experienced Hospice nurses, which provided a new perspective into the dying process and taught us how the dying can communicate with us if we learn how to pay close attention. We all began listening to my mother's "incoherent babbling" with new ears and heard what turned out to be some comments with amazing portent.

Mother began sleeping most of the time and was unable to verbally communicate by the seventh day at home. She blurted out some things like "7-11" and "Does anyone here speak Italian?" Those who witness this process may not understand and may say things like, the brain "is dying," or the drugs are "making a person hallucinate," or people are "talking out of their heads." We realized, however, after thinking on it that perhaps she was trying to communicate in some way with her grandmother, the monolingual Italian woman who was Nina's nurturer in her childhood and perhaps Grandma Lawrence was in the room to help my Mother "cross over." The numbers Mother spoke were incredibly significant. It was the date she would die.

As the hours went on, we began to openly discuss our hope that my Mother would just go and no longer suffer. We all thought she was in physical pain. As a former Hospice nurse who has been present during many other death experiences, I now believe that during our final days, each of us must work out whatever we have left to work out, and many of the "unintelligible mutterings" of the dying have great meaning and significance to those present. What I have come to know is that my Mother was suffering, but not in ways medication could help. Dying was having some degree of suffering and her suffering was very different from physical pain. Mother was working out some unresolved life issues before she left this world. I now feel we all do that on some level during our dying process.

During those last days of Mother's life I found myself getting up in the middle of the night whispering things in her ear that I wanted her to know (as hearing is the last sense to go) in case she died during the night. Each night I would lie in bed and as I would remember things I wanted to tell her, I would tip toe into the living room, being careful not to awaken anyone, and whisper softly in her ear.

I asked for her forgiveness for all the undue worry, suffering, and pain I had caused her. I told her how much I loved her and had forgiven her for all the mistakes she had made with me, for all the times she lashed out at me in anger when she was angry about something else. I told her how I knew Gregg had also forgiven her and that he knew she was doing what she thought was the best for me at the time. I reminded her how remarkable her resilience had always been in the face of failure and what a great example she had been to me and that she was one of the biggest reasons I had become a successful person. I told her that she had become my role model of how to face and live with cancer and how her incredible strength, courage, and faith, filled me with my own. I also said I knew she was afraid, but that she was facing death with courage and dignity. I told her I hoped I would be able to face my own death with half the courage she demonstrated. She never once responded to me but I know at that point, we were speaking the language of the heart.

Mothers move us emotionally like no others can. They love us and hurt us more than anyone else. They mold our personalities and ultimately form the type of people we become, whether we acknowledge it or not. Let's face it; mothers are our universes for so many years of our lives. After moving through their bodies, we stay a part of them and they stay a part of us, a bigger part than we can sometimes own. They teach us how to respond to people and circumstances around us, whether good, bad or indifferent. They influence and shape us and ultimately, in spite of every attempt not to, we end up much like them.

If you are anything like me, there have been many times across the span of my mother-daughter relationship when I hated my Mother and other times when I pitied her. There were times I loved her like no other, and times I understood her like no one else could. There were times when I desperately wanted her to understand and support me and she didn't, or couldn't, or wouldn't. There were times I needed her and she was there for me, and other times when it seemed as if she could care less. When something important happened in my life, she was either the first person I wanted to tell, or the last. It wasn't until the last few years of her life that I was really able to see her and accept her for whom she was and who she would never be, and love her regardless.

Even after we reach adulthood, mothers still influence how we move through the world. To lose them is not like any other loss we experience because the only person who has known our life history from conception to who we are now dies with them and unless we have it down on paper, our history dies too. One must become ready to face not only the loss of this significant parent, but to also face this unexpected inner death of part of the self. My experience has been that we are forever changed.

Eight days after bringing Mother home, I woke and took a brisk walk as I had been doing my entire stay with my parents. I had breakfast with my sister and dad, and we all began to pray that my Mother would go soon. We were suffering more than she was at this point, and we didn't want her to stay on our behalf. As the hours wore on, I began to tell my Mother she could let go of this life and we would all be OK after she was gone. We would hurt like hell, but we would take care of each other. I told her my sister and I would watch out for Dad and make sure he was taking care of himself. Gently I asked my Dad and sister if they could let my Mother know it was OK for her to go, as I began to sense she was trying to hang on for all of us. Sobbing uncontrollably, they both said goodbye. My sister and I began to sing some of her old favorite songs and read her favorite prayers to her. Nina seemed to become more peaceful.

Around 5:00 p.m., as the blistering Louisiana sun finally began its decent into the murky horizon, Mother's breathing became extremely labored. Everyone kept looking at me to help her; I was willing to take on that responsibility. My Mother's baby was helping my Mother give birth to her physical death and spiritual birth.

Determined not to let her experience a painful death, I gave Mother increasingly more morphine. There was some part of me that also felt I was trying to ease her transition and help her die if I had to. I was very conflicted, but I knew I would not let her suffer so I kept giving her the morphine. This was a decision I would later have to confront in working through my grief.

Around 5:15 p.m. a church acquaintance of my parents, stopped by. This young man had, only weeks before, lost both of his parents in a fatal car accident. I was reluctant to let this person, whom I didn't know, come into the house as it seemed Mother was about to die, Dad motioned him to come in and pray with us.

We were all gathered around Mother's bed as she had begun to breathe very irregularly. We knew it wouldn't be very long. I had read in *Final Gifts* that the dying person often orchestrates who is with them when they go. I thought because I was always my Mother's baby, that maybe she didn't want me by her side when she died. I announced that I was going to the bathroom and left the room. I quietly listened from the nearby laundry room, when suddenly the young man yelled at me to come quickly. I watched as Mother's mouth began to gulp for air, her chin moving in exaggerated gulping motions seemingly trying to get in another breath. I now know it is called "fish out of water" breathing and is an awful term and extremely uncomfortable to witness for the inexperienced. Mother's eyes were partially open, but not seeing. Her chin movements became less and less noticeable and finally stopped. I put my ear to her chest and heard a faint irregular heart beat. As my head rested on my Mother's chest I noticed the room was deadly quiet. Everyone was holding their own collective breath. I again listened intently, and there was only silence. I raised my head and said, "She's gone."

After what had to have been just a few seconds, I really couldn't believe she was no longer there, so I put my ear to her breast one last time. Again there was only silence. I looked at my Mother's face and I could see that Nina; mother, wife, grandmother, and great-grandmother, incredible woman, and so much more, had left us. It was starkly clear that only her physical shell was remaining.

The young man who couldn't be with his own parents when they died was given the gift from my Mother of being with her when she died. The daughter who could never take responsibility for her own life (me) had the utmost responsibility at her mother's passing - strong lessons for us all.

There is a ritual that follows death that is seldom acknowledged. This is what I call the "busyness" or business of death. There is so much to do - paperwork of all kinds, a memorial or funeral to plan, insurance companies and banks to notify and the list goes on and on. It can sometimes take several weeks; therefore the true shock of death doesn't even set in until all this death business is finished.

I remained in shock for three to four months, feeling a numbness I had never felt before. I thought I was functioning, but realized later, I was walking through the motions of life, but not ready to feel the intense pain that was to come. I also struggled for months to feel something from my Mother. I felt that because we had been so closely intertwined that she would let me know; give me some sort of signal that she was alright.

The rest of the summer wore on into fall. I felt nothing from her. No message, no signal, nothing. I began feeling that the "great hereafter, heaven, etc." was all a bunch of man-made crap. I started to experience an emptiness inside that was beyond anything I had ever felt before; truly a dark night of the soul. I went to grief counseling, sobbing out this story for months. I shared with my counselor the intense guilt I felt about the morphine. I shared the anger that all the responsibility was put on me to make these decisions about my mother's care and death. I wept and screamed out in a pain so deep I cannot describe it. Still there was this silence, an intense void. My faith was shaken to the core.

Celebrating Christmas in our traditional way was just not going to happen. My birthday is December 2nd, and December 30th was Mother's birthday. So many of the decorations were handmade by Mother. I just couldn't, in fact wouldn't do it. I felt the pain would be more than I could bear. Rather impulsively we decided to fly to Hawaii for Christmas. There was sun and surf and many beautiful days, but I felt like a robot going through the motions. I just couldn't shake the emptiness I felt.

On what would have been Mother's 84th birthday, we decided to climb Diamond Head. It is a rigorous two hour climb and there were points at which I thought I couldn't make it. Thinking of Mother and the battles she had fought with cancer the past four years of her life, I persevered and got to the top. I am only five feet tall and had to wait awhile for a spot in the front of a very small lookout area. I finally made my way to the iron bars that bordered the lookout. It was an unusually clear day with blue skies and amazing panoramic views of the entire island of Oahu. Still feeling this painful hole in my heart that Mother used to fill, I made a birthday wish for her that she could have lived long enough to be at the top of this incredibly beautiful volcano and witness this majesty of nature with me.

Using my digital camera I began to look for a shot. Out of the corner of my eye, I saw something fluttering. An orange black-dot butterfly, just like the one Cori and I had placed over my mother's deathbed, was flirting with me! She kept fluttering by and seemed to be teasing me into trying to take a photo of her! I said out loud without thinking, "Ok Nina, come on and get in the picture! After all it IS your birthday!" This little butterfly gently landed on a bush of bright yellow flowers right in front of me, unfolded her wings, posing perfectly. I snapped the shot and away she flew!

Arriving home I excitedly loaded the digital photos on to my computer. Viewing them immediately brought up the photo of the butterfly. I had gotten a perfect shot! There she was, bright orange and black, with the distinctive white dots outlining her wings, posing perfectly on these beautiful little yellow flowers!! This was amazing!! I also began to feel something stir deep within me. I could feel my heart beating again, almost racing. I felt a great joy that I had captured this amazing moment.

I began to zoom in and out, cropping the butterfly photo and realized there was something underneath the butterfly that I hadn't noticed before. There, under the foliage, as big as life, was a bird nest with two eggs in it!! At this moment I knew I could again rejoin my life. I knew my mother had waited to give me these very special gifts on her birthday. The first gift from her was that she would always be a part of me - as I was in her- so she was in me. The second gift was the message that in loving deeply, heartbreak and loss will happen, but there is always new life and with new life comes renewed hope. Nina's third gift to me was to convey one of the great mysteries of life. Life is full of surprises (which she loved) that while mystifying us, can renew our faith and bring us back to fully appreciating the gift each moment of life truly is. And when a gift is given to you, you may want to examine it a bit more closely as there may be an extraordinary moment you could miss.

I still feel deep pain over the loss of my Mother as the three year anniversary of her death just passed.

Writing this story has helped me revisit that amazing experience of being the midwife at her death, just as if it had happened yesterday. Time often brings perspective, and I can truly say there are now days when she doesn't cross my mind. Some days are still difficult to get through without tears. But now instead of looking for signs outside of me, I hold my Mother in my heart. Planting many butterfly plants in my back yard, I can watch the comings and goings of many butterflies and continually be amazed at the depth of what I don't know.

I now see my Mother's passing and my presence there as a great honor she bestowed on me. It brought out my deepest strengths, made me face my greatest fears and sorrows, conquer them, and opened me to sharing gifts of my own with others. Nina's death helped me to further come into myself as a woman. I have become more fully who I am without internal judgments. I am learning how to simply be me. I also continue to learn the lessons of faith and try not to miss what is happening in each moment.

My sister passed away four months ago, in New Orleans, from cancer in a remarkably similar manner as my Mother. I was at her bedside as well, and laid my head on her chest and heard her heart stop too. Everyone has sent me condolences for my sister's loss in butterfly cards and notes, and butterfly magnets now crowd the front of my fridge. I even have a few butterfly pins that were my mothers' and have proudly taken ownership of being the newest "butterfly queen" in our family.

Grief is an individual process that we all go through in unique ways. Whether we take comfort from faith, family, friends, counselors, or in butterflies, the important thing is to go through it. Be gentle with yourself and know this process takes whatever time it takes.

Know that as you face your own pain, there are those of us out here that have gone through this trial by fire and have emerged as more whole human beings with a greater relish for life… Kind of like a butterfly breaking free of its cocoon.

Take good care, and when you see a butterfly, think of our Nina.

ABOUT THE AUTHORS

Jayne Emmitt Andron *is a Bereavement Counselor in the Philadelphia area with Hospice and Palliative Care/The Home Care Network of the Jefferson Health System. She is a graduate of Belmont University in Nashville, Tennessee and of Villanova University, Villanova, Pennsylvania, with a master's of science in Counseling and Human Relations. The mother of two sons, she and her husband live in Wayne, Pennsylvania. She can be contacted at andronj@aol.com*

Arianna *is a goddess, a seeker, a nurse and eternal spirit. A boomer born in 1954 she is a divorced, single mom, now with a grown professional daughter. After a first time degree in communication, she went back to school for an ADN, BSN, and then Masters of Science in Nursing. She is a holistic nurse and a spirit living an earth adventure ... believing every day is giving her a new experience in learning how to love in the world of form. Arianna can be contacted through Carole Ann at: ca@livingthepresence.org*

Elizabeth Bachofer *lives in the magnificence of the moment. Presently residing in Kansas City, MO she assists herself and others in realizing universal truths as expressed in their lives. Living Presence in the business world is a strong focus for her. Her easy, light manner coupled with her refreshing clarity brings forth words of deep understanding. Her networking abilities enhance Conscious Awareness Inc.; her sense of community enlivens gatherings. Elizabeth enjoys affirmative prayer treatment work and quietly* *assisting others in living life NOW. She can be reached at happyeliz@hotmail.com*

***Gretchen Reising Cornell**, Ph.D., R.N. is currently a professor at Utah Valley State University, Provo, Utah. As a nurse educator she finds joy in nursing and caring. She appreciates the interconnectedness we share as passengers on this earth. Writing the story of her mother's life and death has caused her to reflect, ponder and process the meaning of being a mother and a daughter. Gretchen is now writing her own story, Better Me, and the story of her late husband as a legacy for her children. She can be reached at cornelgr@uvsc.edu*

***Barbara Dossey**, PhD, RN, AHN-BC, FAAN, is internationally recognized as a pioneer in the holistic nursing movement. She is Director of Holistic Nursing Consultants in Santa Fe, New Mexico, and International Co-Director of the Nightingale Initiative for Global Health (NIGH). She has received many awards and is an eight-time recipient of the prestigious American Journal of Nursing Book of the Year Award. She has authored or co-authored 23 books including Holistic Nursing: A Handbook for Practice (5th ed., 2008), Florence Nightingale Today: Healing, Leadership, Global Action (2005), Pocket Guide for Holistic Nursing (2008), Holistic Nursing (30 interactive web modules (2005), Compassionate Care of the Dying: Manual and Standards for Practice (2004), Florence Nightingale: Mystic, Visionary, Healer (2000), and AHNA Core Curriculum for Holistic Nursing (Editor) (1997). A major focus of her work currently is holistic and integral nursing, compassionate care of the dying, and virtual education. She is also exploring the impact of Florence*

Nightingale's life and work on contemporary nursing and humankind. For more information see web sites: www.dosseydossey.com and www.NIGHcommunities.org

Carole Ann Drick, *DNS, RN is an international speaker on Simplified Spirituality and Living in the Present Moment. Opening to non-dual wisdom in 1989, she continues to ask the question, "Is it possible to live in the present moment without the influence of the past?" She daily discovers the answer. She is the Founder/Director of Conscious Awareness Inc., Austintown, Ohio and facilitates individuals, groups and organizations in Living and Healing in Presence. She has numerous lay and professional articles on spirituality, intuition, and holistic healing plus deeply insightful CDs. Carole Ann continues to explore and live from the depths of Stillness observing its effect on the human condition. Her presence is a gentle invitation for each of us to move deeper into the essence of who we really are. Contact her: www. livingthepresence.org*

Mary Blaszko Helming, *Ph.D., APRN-BC, FNP, AHN-BC has been a Family Nurse Practitioner for 27 years. She is currently teaching in the Graduate Nurse Practitioner Program at Quinnipiac University, Hamden Connecticut. She has a special interest in spirituality and healing through prayer. Practicing holistic nursing has become her passion. Mary lives in the rolling hills of Connecticut with her husband, a 14 year-old daughter, a 21 year-old son, and her father. Contact Mary at Maryaprn@aol.com*

Mary Ellen Jackle, *R.N., M.S.N., works in the Neonatal ICU at Johns Hopkins Hospital in Baltimore, MD. She also facilitates workshops on "Caring for the Caregiver:*

Nurturing Health Care Providers and Families", and is a member of the American Holistic Nurses' Association. She lives in Westminster, Maryland with her husband and two cats. E-mail Mary Ellen at rcjackle@aol.com

Kathryn Kilpatrick *began her career as a speech and language pathologist in 1969 after completing her Master's Degree at the University of Massachusetts in Amherst. She specializes in working with older adults primarily in their homes and her experience led to the publication of over 35 products since 1977. Kathryn created Communication Connection in 2000 which provides training on how to enhance communication and connection across the decades with an emphasis on supporting the families, friends and caregivers of those with communication challenges. She created Memory Fitness Matters in 2005 to raise awareness about memory fitness for all ages with a focus on safe independence for older adults. Email her at: kathy@connectionsincommunications.com*

Helen Elizabeth Martin *is a National Board Certified Teacher who taught high school science and mathematics for 32 years. She is a Founding Director of the National Board for Professional Teaching Standards. She is also the Founding President of the Satellite Educators Association. Currently she is retired and teaching a Bible Study at the local YMCA and serving as an Educational Consultant to various academic institutions. She has numerous publications and has recently self-published a commentary on The Song of Solomon, a book of the Holy Bible. Helen can be contacted at: SatTeacher@aol.com*

***Deanna Naddy** resides in rural middle Tennessee, retired from an extensive career in Nursing Education. Within her Health and Wellness Center she has an active holistic alternative health practice. Her three children and twelve grandchildren play an active role in her life. She maintains an intense curiosity for learning and experiencing what life has to offer, exploring different cultures, spiritual beliefs, healing modalities, travel, enjoying family and friends, and coming to terms with her own Inner Presence. Contact Deanna at djnaddy04@bellsouth.net*

***Bozena M. Padykula**, MSN, RN, AHN-BC is currently living and working in Kensington, Connecticut. She came from Poland when she was 18 and never even imagined that nursing would be her life mission. As a nurse she has held two roles during the last four years, clinical nurse III on a geriatric/psychiatry unit at John Dempsey Hospital and Adjunct Nursing Faculty for the University of Connecticut School of Nursing. As a mother of three children, she is married to a supportive, loving man who loves to spend his spare time with family in the RV house. To stay in balance she takes bike rides and long early morning walks on the beach. She has a strong interest in energy medicine and the effectiveness of acupressure as a healing modality for range of daily misalignments. She can be reached at bozenamp@hotmail.com*

***Pam Parsons** was born in New Orleans and feels this is where she got her strong sense of family, her deep love of music, her appreciation of good food, her resilient spirit, and her soulful heart. Her careers have literally spanned a* *lifetime. She was a lay midwife for many years and welcomed hundreds of babies into the world. As a registered nurse, Pam created several teen pregnancy and parenting programs and was an Early Interventionist helping to prevent child abuse and neglect. The remainder of her career has been spent as a Hospice Nurse and a Bereavement Counselor in a community based, not-for-profit Hospice. Pam is married with three children and three grandchildren. She and her family experience great fun doing the many outdoor activities in the mountains and lakes of North Idaho. Pam can be reached at ppmarie@msn.com*

***Susan Swaner**, BS is a native of Middle Tennessee and a mother of three sons, three grandchildren and three marriages. She now lives and travels with her spiritual Partner on their sixty foot wooden sailboat. As an avid meditator and student of Spirituality and psychology, Susan enjoys writing, cooking and baking, swimming, flowers, and group meditation. Presently she is working on her first fiction book relating to her life experiences. Her long term goal is to write a sequel book about their sailboat journey. Gratefully she is living her dream, to stay at home and write, living each moment in awe and wonder! Contact Susan: swanersuzyq@myway.com*

***Rowena C. Buxton Tauber** now lives in Nairobi, Kenya, East Africa, having spent the last 33 years living and working in countries far spread out – Cyprus, United Kingdom, Saudi Arabia, Hong Kong, China, Japan and 20 years in the United States. In addition to the above she has been grateful to travel to many other countries along her way – sometimes with her mother and to many others on*